# Possession of Willowland Manor

*Enjoy!* *Linda Hughes*

Linda Hughes

ISBN: 1522978216
ISBN 13: 9781522978213

# Books by Linda Hughes

Possession of Willowland Manor

Yesterday Forever Gone

Secrets Without Compromise

Cloistered Secrets


Visit: www.LindaLHughes.com

# *Dedication*

## MARGARET MCKENNA O'MORGANS

*Thank you Maggie, our aging West Highland White Terrier, for resting under my desk while I write and quietly keeping me company. Thank you Maggie for taking me outside for much needed walks, so I can clear my mind for the next chapter. Above all, thank you for reminding me of the simple pleasures of life: watching squirrels scurrying up trees, following busy rabbits nibbling on grass, and stopping to smell the roses. Although you may be ninety-six in human years, thanks for reminding me what's still very important like . . . what's for dinner?*

Before beginning a tale of good versus evil, a

wise grandfather would say,

"Never let the truth get in the way of a good story."

# Chapter 1

Mississippi - 1875

Startled from a deep sleep, Kizzi heard the cabin door crash inward. Dazed from the abrupt awakening, a hand thrust a rag reeking of spoiled meal into her mouth. Although impossible for her screams to be heard, she screamed anyway. Gagging and gasping, she thrashed about in the darkness against those who roughly placed a coarse bag over her head. Unable to see or speak, she was yanked from the bed and taken outside into the cool and misty night. When she refused to walk, her captors dragged her through the moist ground, leaving uneven ruts in the earth behind. As mud gathered between her toes, a chill rushed through her body; the damp air wafting through her nightgown and mingling with perspiration trickling down her sides. What was happening? Beyond anything she could imagine, she struggled to understand her dilemma. Where was she going and why? Except for the sounds of heavy breathing and footsteps on each side thumping against the ground, nothing else disturbed the stillness of the night.

Aware of the ground changing from wet to soggy, slime collected on her lower legs, weighting her down even more. Knowing she'd entered the thick willowed section of the plantation—an area considered off-limits and never ventured into—she was besieged with terror. Why was this happening? But even as she questioned, she already knew the answer. Tilting her head to the side, she hoped to breathe easier but turning twisted the bag closer, making it more difficult to inhale.

While nothing was said between her captors—assuming there were two—the dragging finally stopped. Dumped headfirst onto the cold ground, she was unable to protect her stomach, feeling herself bounce oddly to one side. Her muffled screams of pain seemed pointless. Without delay her captors lifted her once more to a standing position. Free for a moment she tried to run into the sinister unknown but was quickly grabbed, pushed to a sitting position, and firmly held there by both shoulders. If only they'd remove the sack and clear her mouth, she helplessly begged to herself. She tried to reach under the sack, but her hands were callously knocked away. Who were these ruthless and uncaring people? Did she know them? Impossible, no one she knew could be this cruel. As their labored breathing somewhat subsided, they began to viciously kick at her legs and feet, most likely to free the clinging clumps of mud and lessen their burden. She whimpered in anguish as pain ripped through her ankles. When the pounding finally ceased, she was awkwardly picked up again. This time, held under each arm and pulled backwards. Even more confused than before, her feet left the ground; her bare heals slapping and scraping against what she thought were stairs, causing horrific shooting pains to engulf both legs. Grunts and groans commenced from her captors as they tugged her upward. Listening to the creaking of the stairs and just in case she had a chance to escape, she tried to reason where she was. Where were these stairs? She knew of no stairs other than those in the big house. Her body resting momentarily on a flat surface, she heard what sounded like a door squeak open. Jerked up and heaved a few feet, she landed on her back, sinking into what felt like dried straw scratching roughly against her skin.

All became silent except for the sounds of boards sagging under the weight of movements near her. Without delay something heavy was pulled over the sack covering her head before stopping and resting around her neck. As it tightened, the realization it was a rope and she was going to be hanged set in. Salty tears tickled down her cheeks, mixing with the mucous running from her nose. Knowing there was nothing she could do to loosen the rope or escape from this dismal situation; she still instinctively reached for her neck, wanting to somehow save herself. In the faint moonlight filtering through the barn's attic door, her thick waist and partially exposed heavy breasts were easily noticeable.

Feeling the rope squeeze into her skin and knowing the end was near, she asked God to forgive her sins and any wrong she'd done others. But what of the wrong done to her by the lord of the manor's son? In a drunken state he'd attacked her in the cellar storage. She'd tried to fight him off, but with no way to escape he'd over-powered her. Cupping his hand over her mouth, he'd slurred the words, "I'll kill you if you speak of this to anyone." Having said nothing to nobody, why was this happening? Again, she already knew the answer.

Just before her body sailed through the air and although her words were not heard, she hollered with all her might, "I curse those here and far who have suffered this injustice upon me. I curse all with sickness and hunger . . . with pain and sorrow. I curse this manor with fire and damnation. Future seed from this family will never prosper or find peace."

As Kizzi flew downward, the silence was interrupted by the settling of the beam holding the coiled noose, a momentary thud as she touched the barn floor, and the immediate crack of her neck. And just as her body stilled, the sun peeked out in the distance and a lone rooster crowed.

After sending his helper away, the older of the two men involved in Kizzi's demise, waited by the back entrance to the mansion. As he requested to see the lady of the manor—even at such an early hour—he knew she would be waiting. In no time at all she appeared.

Hesitantly stepping forward, the man bowed before saying quietly, "Madam, it is done."

Receiving a nod of approval, he waited—but not patiently—for further instructions. After a lingering silence, he asked cautiously and barely above a whisper, "What should be done with her?"

The reply was both immediate and abrupt, "Not my concern. Do whatever is necessary, but she must never be found. She ran away . . . never to return. Do you understand?"

With lowered eyes he stepped backward and mumbled, "As you wish, Madam."

# Chapter 2

William Wayland and his son, Ronald, had been away from home longer than expected. The trip to Natchez should have taken less than a week but instead lasted almost ten days. Although both were negotiating with cotton buyers from the North, Ronald spent the majority of his time visiting the ladies at Little Lill's, a well known house of pleasure.

It seemed of no consequence to Ronald that he was betrothed to the daughter of Stone Bennington, the wealthiest and most influential plantation owner in their parts. But then, nothing much mattered to Ronald except doing as he pleased. Besides, it was his mother's wish for him to marry Sara Elizabeth, not his. He found her boring and demanding; her endless giggling repulsive. Above all, she was too skinny for his liking.

Although it seemed understandable for his mother to yearn for an improved future, it was not his responsibility to make her dreams come true. He was content for his life to continue as it had . . . full of distraction and merriment. After all, his good looks and quick wit had carried him this far without Sarah Elizabeth's money.

But as his mother constantly reminded him and anyone else who'd listen, times had been hard on her during the war years and since reconstruction. She acted as though she was the only one to have personally suffered, compounded by watching her household slaves scurry to the North for better jobs and pay. On many occasions his father argued to deaf ears that she wasn't the only person to suffer loss. Sometimes, his father—in an unusually raised voice—would remind his wife that he didn't have enough field workers to care for the land or pickers to gather the cotton . . . noting half their land—not destroyed in the war—still lay dormant.

Since most of the skilled and productive slaves deserted the plantation during and after the war, those remaining were considered free laborers and provided with a place to stay, food to eat, clothes to wear, and a small plot of ground to tend their own vegetables. In addition to these benefits and even worse, they were paid to work. William Wayland often said to anyone who'd pay him the least bit of attention, "It's a damn shame. The freeing of the slaves has ruined my life."

When the war ended, some ten years earlier, many plantation owners banded together in cooperative ventures to survive, but William Wayland didn't believe in sharing . . . selfishly deciding to keep his cotton profits for himself and his family. The problem . . . each year his profits were dwindling. By next year, he'd be dead broke . . . then what? Even Bennington's influence had traveled to Natchez, hindering his ability to get a decent price for what little cotton his land now produced.

William's original plan was to leave Natchez at daybreak and be home well before dark. But Ronald had not cooperated, having passed out behind Little Lill's; his money and boots unknowingly removed from his person. Not only did it take time to find Ronald but also an extensive search to locate his son's horse. After purchasing new footwear and attempting to sober him up for the delayed ride back to Willowland, William watched his son heave his insides out and cuss about his missing possessions. Knowing full-well it was Ronald's own fault to be in this position; William could only shake his head, wondering why God took his other boys in the war and spared Ronald. Now, all he had left was one daughter and one worthless son. For what Ronald contributed, he might as well of had two daughters, he thought with disgust.

After a hard-pushed nineteen mile ride, they were within the final mile of home. As dust turned to night, William pictured himself sitting on the veranda and holding a sweet tea in one hand and a cigar in the other. Anxious to leave the long trip behind, William slapped Ronald's horse on the rump and kicked his own. Outwardly tiring but familiar with the road and surroundings, both horses easily galloped forward. Entering the plantation grounds and moving along at a steady pace, his son's horse abruptly skidded to a stop, reared, and violently threw Ronald off. Not far behind, William pulled his horse up, jumped off, and ran to Ronald's side.

"Son, are you all right?" he questioned.

Receiving no response, he looked around for options. Even darker under the willow tree-lined canopy of the entry road, it was impossible to clearly see Ronald's face. Was he dead or alive? He did his best to listen to his son's chest but was uncertain if he heard a heartbeat. Removing his gloves, William placed his trembling hands around Ronald's neck. Again, it was unclear whether he felt movement other than his own shaking. Ronald's horse had bolted in the opposite direction, but luckily his horse remained. Now what? No way could he lift him onto the horse by himself.

Although not wanting to leave him crumpled in the dirt like a rag doll . . . perhaps dead or near death, he needed to go for help.

Rushing up the brick steps leading to the front door, he began yelling, "Mother, I need help. Ronald's hurt."

Thrusting the enormous door open with one yank, he was met by Matilda, their oldest house slave—or former slave—and the only help beside Kizzi allowed to reside inside the main building during nighttime hours. As he rushed past her on his way through the manor's bottom floor, he called back, "Matilda, get my wife. I'll get hold of Hans."

Exiting the back of the building, William ran past a cluster of ramshackle cabins, banging on the largest one and yelling for his overseer, "Hans."

Opening the door quickly, Hans answered, "Here . . . Boss."

"Bring a cart without delay. Ronald was pitched from his horse and gravely injured. He might be dead."

"Where? Where is he?" Hans questioned.

William quickly answered, "On the access road just inside the entrance. I'm going back. Make haste!"

As Hans hurried toward the stable to hitch a cart, William's wife, Abigail, stepped outside and called, "William, what's wrong?"

"Ronald has fallen from his horse. I'm coming inside."

Once face-to-face and more composed, he continued, "Be calm, my dear. I don't know how bad it is. I must hurry back to his side. He's within a stone's throw, and Hans will help fetch him."

Before Abigail could ask more questions, William had already galloped away.

# Chapter 3

They carried Ronald into the parlor, the nearest place to lay him down. Hoping Abigail didn't notice, William made no mention of their son's leg dangling oddly to one side. When they placed him on the sofa, he uttered a feeble groan but his eyes remained closed. Hearing the moan, even as slight as it was, Abigail was relieved beyond words her son was still alive. Her worst fear stifled, she awkwardly wiped away the pooled tears below her eyes with a tightly clenched handkerchief and sighed.

"Hans, ride for the doctor in Vicksburg," William ordered. "Tell him he must come immediately. Tell him it's a matter of life and death. Do not take no for an answer."

"Yes, Boss. I'll do my best to be back by daybreak."

Looking at Matilda, Hans growled, "Take his boots off and get warm water to wash the dirt from his face."

Never before answerable to Hans, Matilda looked questionably at Abigail.

"Yes, yes, Matilda . . . I'll help," Abigail responded, seemingly caught in a trance. Questioning how to proceed, Abigail asked, "William, what else can we do until the doctor arrives?"

"Make him as comfortable as possible. I reckon the doctor will tell us what's wrong. If or when he wakes, he can say what's hurtin'."

"Don't tell me "if" he wakes. I cannot endure the loss of another child."

"Mother, Matilda will tend to Ronald. I will be in the library pouring myself a sizeable whiskey. Go upstairs and have Kizzi prepare tea for you and read your Bible."

Abigail's response was hasty and stern. "She's gone. She ran away. I can prepare my own tea."

She could prepare her own tea. Of course, she could. That was nothing compared to doing whatever was necessary during the war . . . and since. She'd gotten quite adept at replacing glorious balls and social gatherings with fund-raisers and meetings to prepare bandages. When the house workers deserted her to seek refuge in the northern Union camps, her day-to-day life changed dramatically. The necessity to assume unexpected responsibilities within the manor was suddenly thrust upon her. While doing without luxuries and coping with shortages of common items like sugar and salt, she had no choice but to carry on. At least Matilda's loyalty had never wavered, having been with her since long before she married William.

Watching her husband leave for the library, Abigail's mind was eased that William didn't inquire about Kizzi's leaving. She wished she hadn't said anything, but it was too late now to take back her words. Hopefully, William wasn't paying close attention because of Ronald's condition.

Kizzi had been owned by them since birth. Strangely, soon after her mother's death in childbirth, William insisted Kizzi be kept and not sold, saying her mother was a good worker and never caused them any trouble. As if to further convince her, he'd argued girl babies paid next to nothing at the slave market. She easily recalled the joy on William's face when he talked about Kizzi laughing as she rode cotton sacks dragged behind numerous cotton pickers. During those times, it made her wonder if William desired another child, especially another daughter. Cared for by Matilda and others until old enough to stay in Matilda's room, Kizzi then became Matilda's inside helper. As the years passed and Matilda's work pace slowed, Matilda eagerly used Kizzi as her own fetch-it person.

Life was easy back then . . . watching their three boys grow into young men as they learned to ride ponies and go fishing. Close in age, the boys had contests to see who could catch the biggest fish; the loser cleaning the winner's fish. Ronald was known to quit fishing if he thought he'd already lost. When their daughter, Teresa Anne, would have a tea party to learn the proper etiquette of tea service, William would often join in. She still remembered his exact words . . . even today, "Might I have two lumps of sugar, my lady?" Then, "Ida Claire . . . now there's no room in the cup for tea." Giggles from Teresa Anne would always follow. Yes, life was easy then, she thought with a lingering sigh.

Watching Matilda scurry out of the parlor and knowing she was alone with Ronald, Abigail left her brief recollections behind and carefully knelt beside her son. As she pushed the hair away from his eyes, Ronald uttered, "I saw her. She spooked my horse."

Ignoring his remark and grateful he was awake and speaking, Abigail said, "Thank the Lord, you're all right. Where are you hurting?"

"My head is pounding something fierce. Maybe if I sit up. Oh, Jesus . . . my leg."

Hesitant to look away from his face, Abigail glanced downward, seeing the material on one leg ripped apart and blood stained. Fear of becoming faint, she couldn't look closer but did shoo the flies away before saying, "Best not move. Hans is fetching the doctor." Starting to cry again, she continued, "Matilda should be back directly. I'll get your father and tell him you're awake."

"Mother, why would Kizzi be wandering on the road after dark . . . and in her nightgown?"

"Don't be foolish. You imagined her. The fall must have addled your mind."

"I know what I saw. She was moving swiftly . . . ah, almost like she flew across the road before me. Tell Father to bring me a bottle of whiskey and to hurry."

While hastily leaving to find William, yet not wanting to leave Ronald, Abigail's concern for her son briefly changed into rage against Hans. "Liar," she whispered under her breath.

Han's trip to collect the doctor would take him some ten miles to the north. Through word of mouth, the Vicksburg doctor wasn't as qualified as the Natchez doctors, but this was an emergency. In order to return by morning, he would need to ride hard in the dead of night. Since the roads were rough and winding, the moon in and out of the clouds, it would not be an easy trip. There was also no certainty the doctor would be in Vicksburg when he arrived. But once he laid eyes on him . . . one way or the other, he'd have no problem convincing the doctor to return with him to Willowland. As expected, he always did as he was told, regardless of the task at hand.

Doing what was necessary without question was the same today as it was when he arrived ten years ago on the banks of the Mississippi . . . the plantation's main house barely in sight. Having migrated from Germany . . . dead broke and alone, he would always be indebted to the Wayland family, thus following their orders without regret. William Wayland once told him, "Hans, showing up on my landing like this, you are truly a God's send."

The war finally over and much of the plantation's land burned; the few remaining workers were attempting to revolt and flee. He'd been hired on the spot, replacing the overseer of color who couldn't control the workers. He neither liked nor trusted the coloreds and once in total control; he enjoyed ordering them around. Sometimes, he whipped them secretly if necessary. As the years passed, the whippings became fewer and fewer . . . then non-existent. If unhappy, the workers were free to up-and-leave without notice . . . and many did at first.

Yes, he'd make sure the doctor would come for William Wayland's son.

At some time during the night, William tried to see how badly Ronald's leg was injured but found it impossible to remove the material without causing his son more pain and perhaps more damage. In the early hours of the next day, Ronald—bordering on delirium—was brought to tears by the excruciating pain, often screaming out incoherently.

When the doctor finally reached Willowland by carriage, the blood had soaked through the sofa cushion and onto the floor. Taking one look at Ronald, the doctor sternly said to William, "Have your wife leave the room." The doctor gazed momentarily at Abigail before looking back at William. Keeping her eyes fixed on Ronald's face, Abigail answered, "I cannot leave him."

"Abigail, you must do as the doctor requests," William replied. You've been up all night. You're tuckered out. Please look after yourself while the doctor administers to Ronald."

Wondering if her legs would keep her upright when she stood, she walked away meekly without uttering another word. Besides, she was too tired to argue. Should she seek Hans out? No, not yet. It was more important to wait for news of Ronald's wellbeing.

The hours slowly passed since the doctor's arrival and although exhausted, Abigail could not relax enough to keep her eyes closed. Without knowing how Ronald was doing or what was happening, it seemed impossible to fall asleep. While pacing back and forth along the hall above the stairs, she watched Matilda come and go from the parlor several times. One time when Matilda noticed her, she called out, "Massa says youse mussend goes into the parlor." Abigail did not bother to answer. William had already forbade her from coming downstairs, promising to come to her with information about Ronald's condition in due time.

After the doctor's departure, William quietly entered Abigail's bedroom. Approaching cautiously in case she was sleeping, he whispered, "Ronald is resting in his room. The doctor is hopeful he will live. The sad news . . . his leg has been removed above the knee."

As if she'd swallowed rotten meat, Abigail jumped from the bed and ran to the chamber pot, gagging with each step. "Couldn't the limb be saved?" she asked. "What kind of doctor is he? I don't understand. He only fell from his horse."

"He was a doctor during the war. He said the leg was damaged beyond repair and looked like it had been shattered by a bullet. Luckily, he brought morphine." Clutching the armrest of the nearest chair, William uttered, "Abigail, I need to sit down."

"I must go to him," she exclaimed.

Gingerly taking a moment to settle onto the small seat cushion, William was unable to immediately respond. When he looked up, Abigail was already gone. However, he did say to the empty room . . . right before beginning to snore, "He'll be asleep and won't know you're present."

The next few days were spent following the doctor's instructions and keeping Ronald as comfortable as possible. Consuming their every waking moment, Abigail and Matilda worked diligently day and night to care for him. While dressing Ronald's leg with red oak bark, sweet herbs, and green wormwood, not much else entered Abigail's mind. The doctor promised to return in a week, so her only concern was to keep her son alive and nurse him back to health. There would be time at a later date to worry about how Ronald could get along with only one leg.

Abigail still had not dealt with Hans nor laid eyes on Kizzi. She also had not told William about the problem with Kizzi, or what she'd ordered Han's to do. Her reasons for not telling William were twofold: partly because she'd been caring for Ronald but more likely because she wasn't exactly sure what to say. Perhaps if Kizzi never returned to Willowland, there would be nothing to tell. After all, she just wanted to be shed of her to avoid embarrassment to the family. There was no telling what Kizzi would do or say if she came back with a Wayland child in her arms. After the freeing of the slaves, times were different in so many ways.

On the fourth day following Ronald's operation, Abigail sent word to Sarah Elizabeth, stating he'd been gravely injured, and asking the messenger to wait for a return answer. The reply was not the one she'd hoped to receive.

> *Sarah Elizabeth is visiting family in Vicksburg and plans to return in a fortnight. We see no reason to worry her unduly or ruin her visit with bad news. Our best wishes for Ronald's speedy recovery. Respectfully, Stone*

What a slap in the face, Abigail mused. At one time she'd considered their families equals, especially when her father was still alive. Since Ronald was her only hope to return to the good times of social living and luxuries again, now what would her future hold? She had so desired to have her life back to the days before the war started . . . a time when forty or so slaves worked at Willowland Manor. There were house slaves, drivers, skilled and unskilled field workers, and two head men to oversee the hoeing, picking, and transportation of the cotton. She'd tried so hard to make this union happen, assured once Ronald was Bennington's son-in-law, all would be right in her world again. Although exhausted, Abigail couldn't seem to control her mind from dwelling on the past or worrying about the future. So much to think about and so much to do.

Abigail was fairly certain Hans would not dare say a word to her husband. Long before the deed was supposed to be done, she'd put Hans on notice to keep quiet if he valued his position. She also reminded him William would take her side and believe her above anything or anybody . . . no matter what. After all, Willowland was her inheritance, and William would be beholding to her forever.

Perhaps she should have told William what she saw when it first happened. He'd probably have said, "Boys will be boys." But then, William had always been oddly protective of Kizzi, even defending her childish antics around the house throughout the years.

She closed her eyes to sleep but was drawn back to that night eight months ago. When Kizzi took too long to fetch the supper wine from the cellar, she'd sought her out, hearing questionable sounds coming from downstairs. Curious to see what was happening, she'd hid behind a curtain to watch. To her amazement Ronald stepped out of the cellar door, adjusted his hair with his fingers, and stumbled out the backdoor. Afraid of what might have transpired, she waited until Kizzi stepped into the kitchen. Appearing disheveled and dirty; her blouse ripped open, Abigail grabbed the wine bottle and sent Kizzi to straighten herself. Five months later and noticing Kizzi's stomach growing, she'd told her to no longer be in the house when either Master Wayland or Ronald was present. Also, she was to move from the big house to one of the vacant cabins. Although unspoken, Abigail was determined no darky baby would sully the Wayland name. And even though Matilda was attending to her duties at a slower pace and obviously missing Kizzi's help, she never mentioned the change in arrangements or complained. However, sometimes she caught Matilda and Kizzi in whispered conversations which stopped when she approached.

Both William and Ronald were oblivious to any of the specific household duties or what preparations were necessary to run the inside of the manor. Luckily, neither seemed to have noticed Kizzi's absence during the last few months but did notice when a garment wasn't cleaned properly or a meal not prepared in a timely fashion. Perhaps William was more than usually preoccupied with the decline in their cotton production to notice anything else, becoming quieter and quieter with each passing day. Ronald had not mentioned Kizzi's name until the night of the awful accident.

She had forgotten to ask William if his trip to Natchez proved successful. Perhaps she would inquire tomorrow and also speak to Hans. Then what? Oh, how she hankered for a good night's rest.

# Chapter 4

*I*t was in the early hours of the following morning when Abigail was awakened by Ronald's blood curdling screams. As if wakened from a terrible nightmare, she struggled to clear her head before running to his room.

"God help me. Look at my leg," Ronald screeched.

Not far behind, William appeared. "What's wrong?" he asked.

"Look at it. I must have hit it in my sleep. Look at it. It's opened up."

"Dear God, maggots," William uttered.

Quickly looking away, Abigail said, "I'm going be sick."

"I'll fetch Matilda. She'll know what to do," William offered.

With the help of morphine and Matilda's knowledge, Ronald somewhat settled down. Although a sickening sight, the maggots did not surprise Matilda. She'd cleaned many smaller injuries before on both humans and animals. After removing the visible maggots, Matilda poured something thick and smelling of kerosene over the stump before dressing it again with the previously used herbs.

Two days later, the doctor arrived as promised. By then Ronald had been in and out of consciousness. And even though his forehead felt hot to the touch, he shivered with chills. Constantly babbling and making no sense, seldom did he recognize anyone.

Beside herself with worry and regardless of what the doctor or William said, Abigail refused to leave Ronald's bedside. She listened while the doctor talked quietly and directly to William. Unable to tolerate being ignored any longer, Abigail asked, "Doctor, would you speak up? I cannot hear a word you're saying."

The doctor paused a moment and cleared his throat. "I was explaining to your husband that the area above the wound is red and purple. The problem is not from the maggots but rather from the blood being poisoned. The maggots have merely removed the dead flesh. The best approach at this point is to clear out the poisoned blood. In my humble opinion he needs to be bled." Looking again at William, the doctor asked, "Do you know if leeches can be found in the marshy area by the river?"

Abigail also looked at William, who looked confused but answered, "I will find out. If not, then what should be done?"

"It will be necessary to cut him in certain places to drain the bad blood."

"Doctor, will this procedure make him well?" Abigail asked pathetically.

"I'll not beat around the bush. I know you are craving better news but if I cannot rid him of the foul blood, it doesn't fare well for him."

Right before leaving, having successfully drained much of Ronald's already weakened body of blood, the doctor told them, "I've done all I can do. I'm afraid it's now up to the Almighty."

Handing Abigail a small bottle of opium, he said, "If all fails, perhaps this will make his passing easier."

Later in the evening while Abigail sat alone by Ronald's bed, he woke abruptly. Recognizing her, he said, "Mama, I need to confess what I did to Kizzi. She visited me last night and said it was my fault she'd been cast out."

"Balderdash. You've had a bad dream. Kizzi ran away," Abigail answered sternly.

"Mama, she was at the window and in her nightgown again."

"Ronald, listen to me. That is impossible. She could not be there. You must have seen the lining of the curtain blowing in the breeze."

"I tried to tell her I was sorry, but she kept repeating, 'Too late . . . too late . . . too late.' Mama, I asked Matilda why Kizzi ran away."

"And what did Matilda tell you?" Abigail asked, speaking defensively and becoming uncomfortable with the focus of their discussion. While listening intently to Ronald's every word, Abigail looked around to see if anyone could hear their conversation.

"Matilda shook her head and said, 'I cannot say.' Mama, did that mean she was afraid to answer or didn't know?"

"Ronald, you must only think about getting well. That is all that matters."

Ronald closed his eyes and quit speaking, seemingly lapsing into a deep sleep. Feeling hopeful, Abigail concluded his recognition of her and resting comfortably were both good signs of improvement.

However, just as the sun peeked out the following morning, Matilda entered Ronald's bedroom, finding he'd just passed. Looking closer to be sure he was gone, Matilda heard a distant rooster crow.

When William woke Abigail to tell her the bad news, she shuttered and closed her eyes again, trying to escape the reality of utter sadness. "Rest my dear. I will send news to Teresa Anne. We can discuss funeral plans when you are more able. I do not mean to be harsh, but his body is in poor condition, so arrangements will need to be carried out soon."

Traveling by train and carriage, Teresa Anne and her husband arrived from southern Arkansas by late afternoon. Abigail had already started on the necessary preparations, commenting several times how she'd been unable to provide their other boys with a proper funeral. Telling William, "At least Ronald will lay in the family plot instead of a stone marker with a name, date of birth, and presumed date of death above empty ground." It had always distressed her to know they were placed in a mass grave at Champion Hill. Although it had been twelve years, she never felt as though she could properly mourn for them. She would make sure Ronald would be laid to rest in a proper fashion for his trip to the hereafter.

Abigail insisted on cleaning and dressing Ronald's remains by herself—with Matilda's assistance. It wasn't until she carefully picked out his best Sunday attire that she began to cry uncontrollably. Staring at Ronald's trousers and costly alligator boots, she begged William to make it appear as if he had two legs when he was laid in the coffin. When the expensive oak casket was delivered, coins had already been placed over Ronald's eyes to keep them closed; a linen cloth tied around his jaw to keep his mouth from opening. Once resting in the coffin, Matilda placed spices, mint leaves, and cedar chips around his body.

While Abigail and Matilda were busy preparing Ronald's remains, others were rearranging the parlor to receive the coffin by moving the furniture to the side for easy viewing. The piano, mantel, family pictures, and mirrors were all draped with a dark crepe fabric. Theresa Anne was in charge of having the funeral cards distributed before going through other rooms in the house to place black fabric on all pictures, mirrors, and door handles. Finally, she covered the front door handle and door knocker with the same dark material. Once the window drapes were closed and the shutters drawn, the coffin was placed into the parlor for viewing. Teresa Anne and her husband were the first to sit with Ronald . . . keeping his soul company until burial.

When Abigail looked into the parlor, the setting reminded her of her father's funeral many years ago; her son's body resting in the same place in the same room. Although Ronald's funeral would not be as stylish as her father's, it was still the custom for people to stop by and view the body, showing him the proper respect he deserved.

By the time Ronald was carried to his gravesite—nestled among family graves and surrounded by willow trees, Abigail felt emotionally crushed and numb. She barely heard the single bell ringing in her world of silence . . . counting the twenty-six times it rang for each year of Ronald's life.

Returning to the house, Abigail could not remember a single word the preacher said but did recall hearing the dirt splatter against the coffin. Each time she thought about the soil covering the coffin, she knew her third son—like the others— was gone forever. Usually noticing every small detail, she was unaware that the black crepe fabric had already been removed from the outside and inside of the manor.

Before heading straight to her bedroom, she said to William and Teresa Anne, "I am very tired and want to be left alone with my thoughts and memories."

"As you wish, my dear, but our friends and neighbors have brought food. It would be remiss if a family member did not show their gratitude." Looking questionably at his daughter, William asked, "Teresa Anne, will you come and help me thank our visitors?"

"Certainly. Mama, I'll be back to look in on you. You seem more than played out. If you like, I can stay with you in your room."

"No, but would you send Matilda to me?"

Abigail had drifted off and did not hear the first few faint knocks at the bedroom door. As the knocks grew louder, she eventually stirred and said, "Enter." Seeing Matilda approach, she then remembered requesting her presence.

"Matilda, come closer and sit down."

"Did I doos bad?" Matilda asked hesitantly.

"No, no. I want to thank you for your service through the years and helping during these past trying days."

"'Tis my place in life to serve youse and Massa."

"Matilda, have you seen Kizzi?"

"No, Mistress. I ain't laid eyes on her since before . . . since before young Massa gots hurt."

"Think on it. When exactly did you see her last?" Abigail questioned.

"I's wents to fetch her early the day Massa was comin' home, but she's nowhere to be found. I's looks high and low for her. I'm feared for her. I don't thinks she gone 'n run aways. She no leavin' her shoes behind. Only gots one."

"One shoe left behind," Abigail said, trying to understand.

Matilda held up two fingers before saying, "She only gots one matches shoes."

"Now I understand . . . as in one pair."

"Yes'm. Kizzi not run away with no shoes."

"Matilda, did Kizzi tell you who the father of her baby was?"

Lowering her head, Matilda didn't answer. Abigail stood up and pointed her finger toward her before saying, "Answer me this minute."

"I's don't wants to get in troubles."

"Matilda, I will not ask you again."

"She said it was young Massa."

"That's ridiculous. Do you think she told anyone else?"

"I's don't reckon. She nevers fits in with the others . . . being lighters skinned 'n all. She says to me 'cuz she ain't knowin' hows to birth a baby . . . no mammy 'n all."

"You can go now . . . and Matilda, don't fret. I will find out exactly what happened to Kizzi."

Watching Matilda walk slowly from the room—her body slumping from side to side— Abigail realized how old she'd become. That led to wondering just how old Matilda really was.

She couldn't think about that now. Any thinking was too taxing. She'd reflect on it another day.

Standing near the window and although an especially warm afternoon, a sudden cold breeze blew the curtain inward and a piercing chill went through her body.

# Chapter 5

Still wearing her black mourning garments, Abigail watched as William and Hans followed closely behind the string of loaded cotton wagons. Once out of sight, she thought back to the time she'd asked Hans how it was possible for Ronald to see Kizzi before he died.

"Madam, that is not the case. I can assure you I personally took care of your problem." His answer had been curt—bordering on disrespectful—when he raised his voice saying, "Your problem."

Their conversation cut short by William approaching, she'd been unable to ask for specific details.

Nodding to Hans, William had asked, "Abigail, what is so important to take you away from the house?"

"I felt the need for sun on my face. The porch is still cool and damp from the night air," she'd answered demurely, lowering her gaze.

Finding it difficult to broach the subject again with Hans—difficult under any circumstances—Abigail returned to thinking it must have been either Ronald's imagination or part of his sickness. No longer constantly watching for Kizzi to return, she'd not laid eyes on her, and to her knowledge, no one else had either. Better to just let it be. No use discussing any of this with William and no need to open a hornets' nest if one doesn't exist, she thought.

Soon the fall harvest was completed, and William was extremely pleased with the cotton production numbers. In much better spirits he was more talkative, smiled more often, and generally paid more attention to the inner workings of the manor.

Abigail received a letter from Teresa Anne, stating she was with child. "God never takes away what He doesn't give back," she'd written. Since her daughter had wanted a child for a long time, Abigail was pleased for her but didn't appreciate the reference to Ronald's death. Besides, she was certain God would never replace one child with another . . . no matter whose child.

While finishing the letter, William joined her on the veranda. "Do you mind if I sit with you for a spell?" he questioned with an unusual smile.

"Please do," she responded. I have received good news from Teresa Anne. She is expecting a child this coming springtime.

"That is wonderful news. I was afraid it would never happen," William replied with another broad smile.

"Perhaps, we have seen the worst of it," Abigail continued. "Your disposition seems much improved. I noticed many wagons leaving. Many more than I can remember since the war."

"You are right, Mother. September was a good month with little rain, and the weather this month proved perfect for the gathering. Perhaps, our luck has finally changed for the better. We best enjoy the weather before the cold settles in. Speaking of pre-paring for winter, I'm hard pressed to understand Kizzi's leaving. Do you know why she ran away? Did something happen while we were gone to cause her to bolt so abruptly?"

Beginning to tremble, Abigail answered quickly, "I must return inside directly. I do believe I have the vapors. I can already feel the cool air closing in on me."

"You do look a sight poorly. It is too much for you to run the house with just Matilda. I've been watching her of late, and she' obviously having difficulty tending to her duties. Just recently while scrubbing the floor; she all but couldn't get up. I will talk to Hans about a replacement for Kizzi."

"William, has Matilda complained to you?" Abigail questioned with a frown.

With no immediate response she stood quietly, fluffed her black skirt, and turned to leave. Stopping beside William but not looking in his direction, Abigail asked, "Can I choose Matilda's helper . . . this time?"

Ignoring both of Abigail's questions, William finally spoke. "I know Matilda has been with you for years and years, but you must consider the possibility of her passing on. Someone needs to be trained before that happens. Your health is broken since caring for . . ."

"William, I need to go inside."

"Would you be so kind as to answer my questions about Kizzi's leaving before you go inside?"

"Well, I never . . . treating me like I'm hiding sump'n. Kizzi ran off. Nothing else to tell except we're shed of her. She's gone.

William, it's not my place to look to her or know of her where-abouts. Why do you care? She was nothing except Matilda's helper."

"My dear, what are you saying? Are you accusing me of think-ing she was more than that?"

"This entire conversation is making me a tad tired. I've told you I don't feel well. I need to fetch Matilda to discuss supper preparations."

Left with his mouth wide open, William wondered what had just transpired. His immediate conclusion; Abigail knew he'd fathered Kizzi. If not, then it must be his guilty conscious playing tricks on him. He'd been tediously careful not to show Kizzi any preference through the years. What difference did it make that she was half his. Perhaps, it would have been better to tell Abigail from the beginning, but when Kizzi's mother died and she had no kinfolk; he'd weakened. Perplexed as he reminisced, somehow it seemed his obligation back then to make sure she was cared for. It wasn't unusual for the plantation's master to breed his slaves, so why did he hide it from Abigail? If the war had not intervened, slave babies—especially male babies—added property to a planta-tion's assets. Damn war and damn freeing of the slaves, he thought.

Watching the sun go down and feeling introspective, he could only admit to God that he'd been strangely attracted to Kizzi's mother from the first time he laid eyes on her at the slave market. As he moved his hands over her almost naked body—on the pretense of making sure she was fit—it was as if she'd held a spell over him. He knew he had to have her and paid a pretty penny for her too. Another secret he'd not shared with Abigail. Considered prime meat by the marketer, Kizzi's mother had fetched more money for a young female slave than he could ever recall. Supposedly the daughter of a tribal chieftain, the African raiders had killed her father and mother before snatching her away and sending her to America for a well-earned price.

Even as he'd purchased her, his thoughts of bedding her were uppermost on his mind. Smiling, he'd bedded her more often than was necessary to produce an off-spring.

What should have been a strictly business obligation became an immensely enjoyable task. Naturally, he couldn't speak of that with Abigail either or with anyone else for that matter. After super and during gentlemen conversations over cigars and whiskey, innuendos were often bantered about regarding slave bedding experiences, but he'd never felt comfortable about joining into those particular discussions. Somehow, the reality of his actions with a slave mingled heavily with his feelings of enjoyment and disgust.

Returning to the present and leaving his reflections of the past behind, he was more than aware that Matilda's loyalties were with Abigail. However, he'd cautiously inquire if she knew anything about Kizzi's leaving. Before entering the house, he tried to remember when he saw Kizzi last but couldn't.

# Chapter 6

*H*ans had not slept worth a damn during the entire previous month. Although no obvious reason existed, he wondered if it was due to no longer pushing to deliver the cotton to the mill. There was also the possibility his restlessness was caused by worrying about the land's preparation before the next crop seeding.

He took his position as overseer personally, and the continual setbacks encountered along the way had created anxiety from morning 'til night. Plagued by bad weather and worker problems, he was questioned daily by Mr. Wayland regarding his progress. And each day, as he was unable to easily fall asleep, he concluded these latest issues contributed to his difficulty in relaxing at bedtime. But there was something else bothering him. Something else didn't seem right, but he couldn't quite put his finger on it.

Like most nights and although exhausted, Hans found himself lying in bed, staring at the ceiling, and lost in thought. Regardless of his thoughtful wanderings, his mind kept returning to hiring Grover and then letting him go.

Before Grover showed up, they were short-handed for one reason or another. Having looked for additional help for quite some time—expecting a bumper crop—Mr. Bennington kept grabbing up any and all available workers . . . even boating them in from as far south as New Orleans. When Grover came along, he'd neither heard of Bennington nor knew he was hiring. Barefoot, hungry, and desperate for employment, Grover readily joined the workforce and seemed eager to please . . . promising to work hard. It appeared to be a good decision at the time.

Since Grover had been at Willowland for only a short time and had no connection to any of the other workers, he'd purposely picked him to help with Kizzi. However, starting during the last week of cotton picking, Grover was constantly found drunk . . . even to the point of being unable to stand. He'd thought long and hard to determine the best way to discipline him. The old ways could no longer be used. Besides, Grover's situation was complicated due to his assistance with Kizzi. Although nothing was said out loud by the other workers—at least in his presence—they evidently took notice of Grover's lack of contributing . . . causing them to endure additional bent-over time in the cotton rows. Mindful of past reasons why workers would slow down or even quit, he knew he had to do something about Grover and quickly. No matter what, he couldn't allow Grover to meddle with worker moral . . . or worse yet, tell anyone what happened. Unable to locate how or where Grover was procuring the liquor, and fearful he'd spill the beans about Kizzi, the only answer which made sense was to send him packing.

Even as he'd placed Grover on the barge that would take him downriver, the drunken young man of color kept babbling about being watched. The terror in his eyes was undeniable, and his last statement before boarding was daunting, "Watch out cuz the spook is coming for ya." Ignoring Grover and hoping the barge operator did the same, Hans said, "Be on the lookout for anyone sober who's looking for work. Bring me two good ones and my boss will be beholdin' to ya . . . adding a bit of coin to your pockets."

It was a mere three weeks to the day when the same barge operator waved him over to the landing. Hollering, "I gots news of the colored I took to Natchez." Once close enough to speak normally, the operator continued, "He done himself in . . . hanged himself, he did. Crazy as a loon . . . that one. If not paid in advance to take him to Natchez, he could of jumped into the river for gator food . . . for all I'd care."

Hans did not respond to the news about Grover other than to shrug, preferring to show a lack of interest. No matter how his indifference was perceived, he was grateful the operator neither mentioned anything Grover said nor took any of his words to heart. Before leaving Germany as a young lad, he'd seen what alcohol could do to the senses. If not cooked properly, there was no coming back from its destruction.

"I done my best but only brung one back for ya. He swears he don't partake of the bottle. "

"Mr. Wayland is most appreciative of your help . . . even if it be only one." Dropping a few coins into the man's hand, Hans continued, "We've opened another field, so could use more helpers if you find someone along your travels."

Turning to the new worker, Hans asked, "What are you called . . . boy?"

"They call me, Jefferson . . . boss."

"Well, Jefferson. You've arrived too late for picking, but just in time for planting. Follow me."

Hans had a productive week without problems or delays. Spending the entire day assuring Mr. Wayland the fields were ready, he lapsed into a deep sleep soon after retiring. Sleeping heavily, the tapping noise against the window pane seemed far away yet close-by. Dreaming, he was a small child in his room and watching the wind blow a branch against the window. It was wintertime in Germany, and he could feel the cold coming through cracks in the wall. As he stared outside, he watched the wind move the pale snow drifts aimlessly about.

Not sure what actually woke him, but Hans sat up with a jolt. Curiously drawn to the window, he wondered how the dream's tapping sound seemed so real. Perhaps the wind picked up some pebbles and tossed them against the window pane. Still somewhat hazy and afraid the window might be cracked; he squinted through the dirt incrusted glass. Startled by what he saw; a shadow-like figure swooped past the window before seemingly fading into the dense willowed area. Was he still dreaming? Rubbing his eyes for a clearer look, nothing else seemed out of place. Returning to the side the bed, he slowly sat down, leaned over, and placed his head between his hands. What the hell was that all about? The best answer . . . his imagination was playing tricks on him. Perhaps the moon broke through the clouds at that very moment, casting a wavy and peculiar shadow to appear to float by. The tapping noise at the window was nothing more than part of his childhood dream.

Waking earlier than usual the next morning, Han began thinking about his plans for the day, but the experience from the night before wouldn't leave him. The odd vision, coupled with Grover's spook remark, made him wonder if it was possible for Kizzi's ghost to return to haunt him. He promptly chastised himself for even considering such a ridiculous possibility.

Almost daybreak and dressed except for his boots, Hans grabbed a piece of jerky and broke off a chunk of cornbread. Placing the uneaten food on a small table near the door, he pulled on his first boot. As he reached for the second boot, he felt something crawl up his leg. Jumping up to a standing position, he awkwardly tugged the boot off before pounding his foot against the floor several times. Dropping down his leg and scampering away at a fast pace was a huge spider. Grasping the boot tightly, he wacked at the spider . . . missing it on the first try. Taking better aim, the ugly critter was smashed just as it was about to disappear under the bed. Carefully moving it forward for a better look, the clearly prominent hour-glass symbol was crushed inward. Glad it was dead; he hated spiders . . . but not as much as he hated snakes.

Now fully awake, he gobbled down the set-aside vittles and left the cabin, briefly pausing when he passed in front of the window. No time to think about silly dreams or anything else. Time to get busy, he thought.

While supervising the first day of placing the cotton seeds into the ground, the day turned out to be as expected . . . long and especially tiring. It took a set of three people to do each row. One to place a hole about an inch deep every half step; secondly, another would drop two to three seeds into the newly formed hole; and lastly, the third person would cover the seeds and lightly pack the ground. Row after row was tediously planted by several groups until the field was completed. Stopping just long enough to hurriedly eat or for a quick drink of water at several water stations, the planting continued from field to field until the sun was setting. William Wayland had followed closely behind him throughout the day . . . mimicking his orders word for word.

After Hans gave the final orders to halt, pick up, and prepare for the following day's planting, Mr. Wayland began to offer personal conversation. "Hans, each year will be better and better. I'm much obliged for your help in returning my land to past times. Even though most of the workers are the dregs from the bucket's bottom, you've gotten the most out of them."

"Sir, I'm the one who's grateful for the opportunity to serve you and your farm."

Seemingly tired but appearing thoughtful, William asked, "Hans, do you happen to know the present whereabouts of Kizzi?"

Momentarily taken aback, Hans paused before truthfully answering, "No Sir. I do not know of her present whereabouts. Hoping the delay in responding was not noticed, he continued, "Perhaps it would be better to ask Matilda. Kizzi was answerable to her and Mrs. Wayland. One of them would be more privy to her whereabouts than me. I was told she ran away."

Hans knew his answer sounded stupid. By now, surely Mr. Wayland had already asked Matilda and his wife the same question. Was he being questioned because of something Mrs. Wayland told her husband? Uncomfortably waiting for more questions, he was surprised by his boss's reply. "I've asked Abigail but she told me the same thing. Matilda seems too timid to discuss it, but I'm thinking she knows more than she's letting on. If I push her for more information, she is certain to tell Abigail. Then, Abigail will get all riled up and pitch a conniption. I know you don't stick your nose into household comings and goings, but do you know why she ran away?"

Remaining silent and not knowing how to answer or what to say, Hans frowned as in deep thought . . . tilting his head to the side like he was thinking on it.

"Forgive me for burdening you with this discussion," William said softly. "It's not your problem and not my place to question you about such matters. I'm just hard pressed to understand what happened to her."

"No problem boss. I try to mind my own business and just do my job."

"And a fine job you do. If the next crop is as good as the past one, you'll have more workers and bonus money for your efforts. Good evening."

Nodding, Hans watched William Wayland wearily pull himself up into the saddle and turn his horse toward the manor. Tomorrow would bring another day of planting, and so it would continue until all of the fields were seeded. Once accomplished, they would wait for the right amount of rain . . . not too much or too little. Springtime would turn into summer, and the cotton would grow. Soon it would be picking time again.

# Chapter 7

Satisfied the plantation grounds were problem free with no apparent worker troubles, Hans asked if he could take a couple of days away to tend to person matters.

Readily agreeing with a nod, William replied, "You've earned more than a couple . . . my man. All seems in order here. I will be out and about to keep em busy until your return."

"I'm thinkin' I'll be gone three days at the most . . . leavin' tomorrow," Hans added.

"No problem. Whatever you'll be doing; I hope it fits your fancy."

"Thank you, Sir."

Before going to bed, Hans pulled a small leather pouch from under the bed and packed several necessities into it. Saving the most important item to pack last, he removed the money from a hidden-away tin and carefully buried it inside the pouch. Pleased with the results of his efforts, he laid out the best of his ragged apparel and brushed the dirt from his boots. Too ashamed to tell Mr. Wayland why he needed to get away; his boots were falling apart, his clothing in tatters, and he'd not had the pleasure of a woman in two years.

Awakened in the early hours—about two o'clock in the morning by loud thunder—Hans wasn't expecting rain, especially before leaving or while away. The days had been clear and warm with no hint of a storm coming. Although rain would be welcomed, a heavy rain with rough winds would not. Even though the young cotton plants were healthy and growing nicely, they were not strong enough yet to endure a bad storm of heavy rain and wind. Best go outside and see what's happenin', he thought.

Barely through the cabin door, a flurry of cold air encircled his body. It lingered for a moment before slowly moving on. How strange for summertime, he thought and shivered. That was almost as odd as the flimsy shadow moving past the cabin's front window. On second thought, he was standing in the very spot where he saw it. Frowning, he looked upward at the night sky, noticing there was no moon . . . only menacing dark clouds.

While mulling over the present and past strange events and having no sensible answer to either one, he turned his head in the direction of the last thunder, waiting to see exactly where lightening would brighten the sky again. When it let loose, he was shocked by its closeness and stronger than he'd originally believed. Mesmerized by the lightning cutting into the darkness—like branches of a leafless tree—he had a foreboding feeling an awful thunderstorm was on its way, possibly bad enough to harm the entire crop.

Beginning to sprinkle and realizing it would be only a matter of minutes before it started raining, he quickly returned inside. Feeling guilty about the animals in the barn and adjoining stable, especially the horses, it didn't seem right to go back to bed. Unlike the mules, the horses became skittish and restless when it thundered. Listening to the wind pick up and knowing the barn doors and shutters were wide open, he grabbed a hat, hurried outside, and banged on the nearest cabin doors . . . hollering for Jefferson and three others to shut and bolt the openings. Following closely behind to make sure all of the doors were securely closed, Hans sprinted back through the downpour to his cabin. Although knowing some of the cabins leaked terribly, he didn't care . . . his didn't.

As he speculated about how bad the storm would eventually be, the wind and rain suddenly stopped. Relieved it was over and not as expected, Hans sighed. Not only did it become calm outside but eerily still. There were no frogs croaking, no crickets chirping, and no birds calling. Usually after rain, the animals were abuzz with chatter. Now what, he questioned.

Wanting to get back to sleep . . . even for an hour or so before his busy travel day, Hans removed his soaked boots and wet socks. Just as he stretched out and thought about his plans for tomorrow, a flash of light illuminated the entire room—as bright as midday—followed immediately by a violent boom. Jumping up and bounding to look outside, he could already see flames coming from the center of the willowed area. Since the old slave barn was the only structure in the area capable of producing that much fire, he assumed it was hit by lightening. Full of dry straw and rotting timbers, it was no wonder it was burning so rapidly. Even though he watched the billowing flames rise upward for merely seconds,

Kizzi's body hitting the barn's floor flashed though his mind several times.

The unused barn's burning would not be a loss for the plantation, but it would be awful if the old willows burned. Worse yet, it would be horrible if the fire spread to the cabins, the present barn, or God forbid . . . the manor house.

Leaving his cabin for the third time, Hans realized it was raining again. This time, he yelled for all of the workers to come out and help.

Barely heard through the wind gusts and rain, Hans ordered, "Grab shovels and follow me." As they passed the stable and presently used barn, both seemed quiet inside.

With the rain pouring down and no moon, it was difficult to move through the thick low-lying trees, but as they approached the fire, light from the flames lit their way. Close enough to feel the heat, Hans shouted, "Do not go any further. Watch for fire that moves to a tree and pitch dirt on it. If that happens, give a shout out."

Watching the barn burn, Hans remembered what the building was like when he first arrived at Willowland. It was not noticeable from the river . . . hidden out of sight among the trees and not used since slave days. New slaves were first taken to the barn for observation before placing them with the other slaves. It was full of chains to hold and punish those who acted out or misbehaved. When he first curiously went into the barn, the whips and restraints for different offenses were still hanging on hooks in plain sight. Understandably, when the slaves were freed, they refused to go near the barn . . . considering it an evil place.

Damn, his trip away would need to be postponed. That meant replacing his boots would also need to be delayed. Disappointed, he looked down at his toes sticking out of the leather on both sides.

From somewhere behind him, Hans heard William Wayland calling his name. Answering, "I'm here boss," Hans still could not see him.

Steps away and before they were face to face, William asked, "Did the structure get hit by lightening?"

"Yes, it appears so," Hans replied.

"I thought it was a different sound from thunder."

"Boss, is there anything we can do except keep it from spreading?" Hans asked but already knew the answer.

"Nothing to do but watch and hope for the best," William answered.

By the time the rain stopped, the barn had been leveled to the ground, but the immediate surrounding trees were only slightly singed.

Eased when the few remaining embers were doused, William was both eased and thoughtful. Turning to Hans, he quietly commented, "It's probably best the barn is gone. It was no longer of any use . . . just a reminder of days gone by."

Without thinking, Hans asked, "Good or bad reminders?"

"A good question to ponder," William replied, looking pensive. His thoughts—his secret thoughts—were about touching Kizzi's mother for the first time and how much he desired her.

"Sir, I'll not be leavin' tomorrow. It'll be best to cancel my travels for the time being. This mess needs attending to and the fields need to be checked for damage. I'm hoping they fared better than the barn," Hans stated.

With no disagreement from Mr. Wayland regarding his staying, Hans gave final orders to the men to continue to watch for hot spots. As Hans and his boss parted, daybreak broke through. Somewhere off in the distance a rooster crowed.

# Chapter 8

*N*ot long after sunrise and using the backdoor leading into the kitchen, William entered the manor. Matilda and her new kitchen helper were already preparing bread and the smell of bacon permeated the room.

"Is youse wantin' to eat?" Matilda asked.

"Perhaps soon."   Standing hesitantly by the door, William sighed before asking, "Is my wife up and about?"

"No, Massa. She still sleepin'."

"Then, I'd be obliged for a piece of fruit pie and tea," said with noticeable relief.

"Where's youse wants it . . . the dinin' place?"

"No.   Would you mind if I stay here in the kitchen and talk with you while I eat?"

"Massa be more comfort aways from all these goin's on . . . I'm thinkin'."

"The old barn in the willows burned down this morning, so I'm thinking it's the perfect time for us to visit.  Don't you?"

Appearing confused, Matilda replied, "Don't rightly knows what's to be sayin' bout that."

Deciding it was now or never, William asked, "Matilda, do you have knowledge of Kizzi's whereabouts?"

Before replying, Matilda glanced briefly at the kitchen entrance and then at her helper. "Is youse askin' me iffin' I knows where Kizzi be?" she inquired quietly. When William nodded, she shook her head and continued. "I's not looked on her since before youse and young Massa comes home . . . naught one time. Maybes youse knows sump'n?"

"Matilda, if I knew something, I wouldn't be asking."

"Mistress says she'll find out but ain't sayin' to me nothin'."

"The pie . . . please," William requested.

"Yes, Massa."

"Did you talk much with Kizzi's mother?" he asked, taking his first bite of berry pie.

This time, she nodded before saying, "Wes tend the chickens. I feeds 'em. She gots the eggs. Sometimes snakes in the nests. I no like snakes. She do."

"Interesting. Why was that?"

"Says her mammy a Priestess of Voudon."

Frowning, William remarked, "Voodoo."

Looking toward the door again, Matilda nodded and continued as if glad to talk. "Yes, Massa . . .Voudon. I's sayin' cuz Kizzi's mammy says her mammy a priestess, and she grows up with snakes before taken by bad men."

"Hmm . . . you know Voodoo is forbidden."

Dropping her head, Matilda said, "I's knows."

Fearing he'd frightened her from talking, William said, "Might we return to Kizzie and to where she may have gone. Did she fancy any of the workers?"

"Massa, sump'n awful happenin' to Kizzi . . . with the baby comin' an all."

"What baby?" William asked, unable to hide his shock.

Before Matilda could answer, Abigail called out from the front of the manor, "Matilda, where are you?"

Receiving no immediate answer, Abigail walked abruptly into the kitchen. Taken aback by the sight of William sitting at the small plank table and eating, Abigail opened her mouth but remained speechless.

Finding the look on Abigail's face somewhat amusing, William smiled and said, "Good morning, Abigail."

"William, what on earth are you doing in here. This is highly improper."

"I'm having a piece of fresh berry pie. It is most enjoyable." Not looking at her, he took another bite, chewed, swallowed, and took a sip of tea. Feeling Abigail's eyes burrowing into him, William finally looked up and said, "I was up most of the night with the storm and the old barn's burning. You must have taken your sleeping potion and slept through it all."

"William, this is not a conversation to have in front of the help. Can we go into the dining room and have a proper breakfast?"

"Of course, my dear."

Abigail turned to Matilda and said matter-of-factly, "Bring our usual breakfast or have your new helper bring it. Makes no never mind . . . but hurry."

"Yes'm."

Following Abigail out of the kitchen, William glanced back in Matilda's direction. He wanted to somehow catch her attention . . .

somehow let her know their conversation about Kizzi and a baby wasn't over. However, Matilda had already turned to her helper and was fussing about the flour being spread out too much.

William and Abigail sat across from each other in the dining room . . . each at the end of the long ornate wooden table. As they made small talk about the weather and Hans cancelling his trip because of the storm, William touched briefly on the old barn burning. But even as he tried to be pleasant, he couldn't help but wonder what his wife knew, even wondering what she was capable of doing. Dear God, what has she done kept going through his mind. Arguing with himself, it didn't make sense for Matilda to say anything if Abigail was involved. And then, Matilda didn't mention "a baby" until after he'd asked about Kizzi fancying a worker. As he discussed mundane information with Abigail, he continued to fixate on numerous questions that were unanswerable.

Dazed himself from lack of sleep, William stated, "Abigail, you look tired and done in. I worry bout you looking drained after a long night's rest. I'm thinking you didn't hear the thunder or the loud sound of lightening hitting the barn."

"William, you are not my father to question my sleeping habits. If you're suggesting the problem lies with the opium; it helps me rest. If I don't take it, I see things that frighten me. Sometimes, I even hear things that frighten me. I take it to escape the things I see and hear."

"My dear, I believe it's the potion causing you to see and hear things."

"William, do not argue with me. I know when and what I see and hear."

"Abigail, you haven't touched your breakfast. Is it not to your liking?"

"I'm not hungry."

"Are you angry because I was in the kitchen talking to Matilda?"

"Don't be silly. Surely you understand the master of the manor does not eat with the help."

"This big house is like a tomb. We seldom talk anymore. You are always sleeping. My children are all gone. I talk with Hans about plantation business, but this is a lonely existence. Can you not see what our life has become?"

"William, you're the one who's tired and talking nonsense. Besides, you're not the only one to have lost children."

"You are right. Please forgive me. Perhaps you should visit Teresa Anne. Be there to help when her baby comes forth. Isn't it about time?"

"Perhaps I shall. I'll think on it."

They finished eating in silence. William cleaned his plate, while Abigail fidgeted with her food . . . moving it slowly around her plate in circles.

William helped Abigail out of her seat before walking slowly to the parlor. Within minutes after sitting, his last thought before falling asleep and snoring . . . one way or the other, Matilda would tell him about Kizzi and a supposed baby.

Following William with her eyes and assuming he was going to the parlor to rest, Abigail returned quickly to the kitchen. She needed to ask Matilda what they discussed. Finding the kitchen helper alone . . . busy pounding and kneading dough with flour flying everywhere, Abigail asked, "Where is Matilda?"

"She no feel good.  Went upstairs," mumbled in a low voice with her head down.

"Speak up.  Where is Matilda?" Abigail quizzed again.

This time in a slightly raised voice, she answered, "She sick . . . went to her room."

"Where is the other new girl . . . ah, Bessie?"

"Fetchin' eggs."

Abigail entered Matilda's room without knocking.  It seemed smaller than remembered, and she also thought it had a window. Reconsidering, the room was once used by her father as a "gentleman's dressing room," so naturally it wouldn't have a window. Standing just inside the doorway, she saw Matilda on the bed in the corner and asked loudly, "Matilda, are you ill?"  With no response Abigail thoughtfully walked farther into the room.  Once next to the bed, she looked down and spoke directly to her. "Matilda, wake up.  Are you ill?"  Still no answer and fearing the worst, Abigail reached down and touched her forehead . . . the possibility of her passing uppermost on her mind.  When touched, Matilda opened her eyes but did not speak.

"What's wrong?  Talk to me," Abigail demanded.

"I's goin' home . . . it's time," Matilda responded weakly.

Placing her hands on her hips, Abigail stated, "You are not leaving me.  What will I do without you?  You've watched over me . . . taken care of me for as long as I can remember." Momentarily looking away, Abigail continued, "Remember when Papa . . . ."  Hearing a soft thud, she quit talking and looked back.  Matilda's eyes were closed; her arm hanging off the bed and resting on the floor.

Every person I have affection for keeps leaving me, she thought and started to cry. Mercy, how could she admit to herself or anyone that she had affection for a slave? Regardless of being freed, Matilda would always be her very own possession . . . given to her since childhood. She lifted Matilda's arm and gently placed it with the other arm over her chest. "What should I do now," she asked . . . almost as if expecting Matilda to tell her. Abigail wiped the tears welling under her eyes, stood erect, sighed, and briskly left the room . . . closing the door behind her.

Seeking William, she entered the parlor. Shaking him several times, it was difficult to rouse him. "William . . . William, Matilda has passed. Will you handle the preparations for me? Unlike with family, I don't know what to do."

"Certainly, but I'm perplexed to know your wishes. Have you given thought to where you want her buried? Your decision will be followed, and I'll not fault your request."

William must have read her mind. Even though she knew Matilda would eventually pass on, she had not come to terms with her final resting place. Abigail answered hesitantly, "The subject was never discussed, but I'm sure she'd want to be with her own people. It is best to lay her with her own kind."

With relief William answered, "Then, it's settled. I'll get Hans. He's seen to burials of workers and their family members before."

Leaving to find Hans, William's disappointment was immense. His distress had nothing to do with Matilda's death but rather the inability to pursue what she'd said in the kitchen. Since Matilda had requested two helpers, she must have known the end was near, he thoughtfully surmised. It was his own fault for not seeking her out sooner. Returning to his previous questions and thoughts, perhaps Abigail was involved. Maybe Matilda wanted to clear the air before leaving. Did Kizzi look like she was having a baby? If so, that would explain why he couldn't remember the last time he'd seen her. Well, I'll not give up on finding out what happened to her. Someone other than Matilda must know the answer.

# Chapter 9

Expecting Hans to be in his cabin, William knocked several times without response. Since Matilda's body needed to be taken from the house as soon as possible, it would be easier on him if Hans would direct her removal. But if that wasn't possible within an hour or so, then it would rest on him to accomplish the task. Without Hans his uppermost concern—after moving her—would be how to proceed. Deciding whether to gather a small number of men or look for Hans, the possibility crossed his mind that his overseer could have gone to the fields to see how the plants survived the storm. That's where he must be, William reckoned.

Seeing Jefferson peeking out of the next cabin's door, William motioned for him to come outside. "Do you know the whereabouts of Hans?"

"No, Sir," he answered shyly.

"Saddle my horse. I'll be in the stable directly."

"Yes, Sir. Right away, Sir."

Returning to the manor to tell Abigail of his plans to search for Hans, he was not surprised to find her asleep in her room. "Abigail, I'm looking for Hans. We will return shortly to collect Matilda's body."

Abigail looked up at him with glassy eyes before mumbling something unintelligible. Disgusted, William left her still incoherent and babbling. Reminding himself not to be angry with her, it was that damn opium. What size bottle did the doctor give her anyway? He should find her hiding spot and throw it out. Reconsidering, sooner or later it would be gone and hopefully by then, her suffering for those who'd passed on will have ceased or somewhat diminished.

As William glanced into the stable, squinting to make sure his horse was saddled and waiting, Hans rode up. His horse was covered with dried mud a good foot above the hooves and when Hans dismounted, William noticed his boots were also heavily caked with mud.

"I was 'bout to look for you," William said.

"I wanted to take a look at the cotton plants before it got dark," Hans answered quickly.

"How did they fare?" William asked with concern in his voice.

"I couldn't get in amongst 'em . . . ground too sloppy. Gave up walking the rows, but the plants are scarcely beat down. Guessin' they'll be alright with the sun's light tomorrow. I'll keep the workers doing other tasks until the ground dries a tad."

"That is splendid news . . . to be sure," William interjected. "But at the moment I need your assistance. Matilda passed in her room and needs to be moved to . . . not sure where." Obviously embarrassed, William asked, "Would you take a handle to it and prepare the arrangements? The mistress and I would be much obliged."

"I'll get on it without delay." Looking toward Jefferson, Hans yelled, "Jefferson, come care for my horse. As an afterthought,

Hans added, "Make sure you clean his legs before putting him away."

Giving a simple, "Thank you," William turned to leave. Stopping, he hollered back in the direction of the stable, "Jefferson, unsaddle and put my horse back too." Noticing Hans had not moved, William said, "It's been quite a time with the storm, the barn burning, and Matilda. Quite a time . . . indeed."

Seemingly unnecessary to comment on Mr. Wayland's remark, Hans inquired, "I'm thinking the mistress is distraught, so will you be in the manor when I bring the men to move Matilda? And, will Madam want to be part of the funeral planning?"

"No, she does not, but she'll have wishes. Of that . . . I am certain. She always does, even when she first declines."

"Should I seek her out or go to you first?" Hans reluctantly questioned.

"Best come to me." William replied quickly. Deciding for the moment that nothing more needed to be discussed, he nodded to Hans . . . as if their business was now complete. As William turned to leave, Jefferson had already taken the reins from Hans and leading his horse toward the stable. Walking away, he couldn't help but wonder if Hans was aware of Kizzi having a baby.

It was a simple task to have four men follow Hans to Matilda's room with William leading the way. They wrapped the bed linens around her body and with two on each side carried her down the stairs. As Hans held the backdoor open, a cold wind caught him and the door—almost knocking him over. Wondering if the storm might be returning, he found his balance before proceeding to a family's cabin used previously to prepare the dead. As was customary for a worker's station, Matilda would be washed before rolling her in cloth and placing her directly into the ground.

As in past burials, somehow the word would get out, and those who wanted to pay their respects could stop by the cabin the following day . . . many coming from neighboring farms if allowed. Usually, the help were buried after dark, so the workers would not be away from their daytime efforts in the field. But since the ground was still very wet, Hans told those directly involved that they could bury her anytime the following day. Even though given the opportunity to choose the time, they preferred to stay with the familiar custom.

When Hans shared the schedule of events with his boss, William replied, I'll pass the information on to my wife to see how it sits with her."

Abigail's first words, "No, no, no . . . that won't do."

"But Abigail, that's the way it has been done for years and years."

"First of all, she needs a casket . . . not just put in the ground without a hard covering."

"My dear, there is not enough time to order a casket."

"Cannot one be made? Surely someone can," she replied pensively.

"I'll need to discuss it with Hans. Is there anything else you desire?"

"Matilda told me there were no gravestones, only bricks and stones to mark the workers' graves. I want her to have a headstone with her name on it."

"I will try my best to see what I can do. It may need to be a wooden cross with her name and date of departure carved into it."

He waited for Abigail to reply but all he received was an expression of despair. With no comment William continued, "Did Matilda say anything else about their graveyard traditions? I've only been present maybe a hand-full of times."

"Another thing she told me was the mourners would place items the deceased used or was fond of on top of the grave's mounded dirt. That way, the deceased can take the objects with them to the afterlife." Barely having the words out of her mouth, Abigail jumped out of the chair and ran out of the room. William assumed she was rushing off to Matilda's room to collect articles for the gravesite. Although he couldn't mention how he felt about the workers' graveyard, fearing Abigail would change her mind, his children buried their pets in a better way.

Within minutes Abigail returned with a handful of Matilda's possessions: a hand-carved back scratcher, a half empty scented oil bottle—a gift from Abigail some five years earlier—a small water pitcher, and tiny doll—made of straw.

"Please give these to Hans to place on top of Matilda's grave. Also, be sure to mention the casket and headstone."

"Abigail, are you certain you don't want to be there?"

"No, I'd feel I was intruding," answered with obvious distress.

Early the following morning and before leaving for the grave-yard, Hans told two men to nail a box together using the set aside wood taken from three of the horse stalls. The light-weight pine had previously been used by Abigail's father to keep the calming goats from escaping the racehorses' stalls.

Shortly thereafter, three men followed Hans to the worker's graveyard. The land, located near the swamp, had been chosen years ago for the slave gravesites because it was considered worthless and not fit for planting. Hans knew from previous burials that most times when a grave hole was opened, it would fill with water. He also knew it would be hard digging in the mud because of the recent downpour.

Abigail slept most of the day and did not eat anything. When not sleeping, she paced through the house, sometimes wandering into Matilda's room. William tried to stay out of her way . . . afraid she would ask for something more. In turn he would need to follow-up with Hans to do something more. Worse yet, what if she changed her mind and wanted Matilda to rest in the family plot.

As dusk approached, William sat on the side porch watching the torches being lit. Knowing the funeral procession would soon be passing by, he decided not to wake Abigail. It seemed cruel to awaken her to the sad sight.

Hearing the door behind him open, Abigail said quietly, "It's almost time . . . isn't it?"

Answering, "Yes, but don't you think watching will make you more distraught than you already are?"

"It will be my last chance to tell her goodbye. That is the least I can do to show my respect to a loyal slave."

William started to argue that Matilda was no longer a slave but to what end. It was not quite dark, so the men carrying the coffin on their shoulders were easily seen. As the coffin passed by, men, women, and children followed behind in no particular order. While uplifted torches showed the way, some chanted, some danced, and others began to sing songs of rejoicing. *"No more pain. No more toil. I'm free to fly. Goin' home to my mansion in the sky,"* repeated over and over.

Full of disapproval, Abigail asked, "Why are they celebrating? This is a solemn time. Not a time for singing and dancing." With no response from William, she realized he neither cared nor understood. Since she was the only person suffering from the loss of Matilda, she needed more of her potion to cope. Leaving in silence, she would find solace in sleep in her bedroom.

# Chapter 10

Hans woke before the sun. With the weather clear and dry, he could finally put the workers back on their regular schedules. And if the weather continued to cooperate, everything would soon be back to normal on the plantation.

He couldn't allow the workers to choose which plants were too damaged to produce, so his immediate priority was to personally point out the ones to pull and reseed. And as soon as the fields were free of problems, he would again ask to leave for a short time.

While barking orders at the women holding onto plows behind the mules, he was already devising a plan to make sure—once and for all—that Kizzi was absolutely dead.

After returning from Matilda's funeral last night, he was again unable to fall asleep. This time, as he tossed and turned, he knew exactly what caused the restlessness. He kept replaying in his mind—over and over—what he saw and was still unable to make any sense of it.

Purposely attending the funeral to make sure the boss's requests were faithfully carried out, he'd stayed behind to see to the filling in of the gravesite and the placing of the wooden cross. Also, per Madam's wishes, he needed to make sure Matilda's possessions were displayed appropriately on top of the mounded dirt. After completion, he would not be responsible if any or all of the objects disappeared.

Having two torches and four men left behind to aid in the grave filling process, he watched the rest of the mourners walk quietly away. Separating his attention from the grave work and the mourners departing for their cabins, he thought he saw Kizzi weaving in and out of their informal pathway. Although especially difficult to see details, her white nightgown seemed to flow effortlessly through the middle of the returning mourners. And even with fewer torches to light the trail back, it was clear enough to see she wasn't his imagination . . . Kizzi was actually there. Was it possible she somehow survived the hanging . . . not to mention the crocodile infested swamp where he'd dumped her body. No, it was not possible. However and in spite of his rational thoughts, Hans found it impossible to concentrate on his duties, continuing to envision the exact spot where he placed her. So, until he had a yeah or nay on what he saw last night, he wouldn't be able to stop thinking about it or get a decent night's sleep.

Hans was never concerned that Kizzi would be found, because no one in their right mind would dare venture into that particular part of the swamp. Although not comfortable about returning there, he would do whatever it took to put this to rest. And just as he'd done after the hanging, he would ignore the congregation of crocodiles and do what needed to be done. Too difficult to do at night . . . more like impossible, he decided that early today would be the best time. Once the decision was made, he'd get on with it . . . the sooner, the better. After giving final orders to the workers and planning to be back before lunchtime, he mounted his horse with a determined look on his face.

Riding straight to the landing, Hans tied his horse to the hitching post before stepping into a small row boat used occasionally for fishing. He would proceed to the swamp, following the same route as before but this time without a body.

Paddling along easily with the river current—making sure to stay close to the riverbank—he traveled a short distance . . . maybe half a mile. With the landing barely in sight, the river turned slightly, creating an occasional overflow when the river rose. It was there that he paddled into the swampy area. Moving gradually inward, he used one oar at a time to navigate through and around the clumps of tall grass. Already in sight, he was aiming for two large willows, partially up-rooted and falling into each other; their roots half sticking out of the water on each side. After reaching the trees, he would have no problem looking into the space where he put her.

Remembering back to being there before and not wanting to draw attention from the watching crocs, he'd lifted her quietly over the side of the boat to avoid a splash. He'd then used an oar to move her under the closer of the two protruding tree roots. Once completely submerged, he'd pushed her down and inward until her nightgown caught on an underwater root. Unable to maneuver her farther in but satisfied the body was tightly wedged; he'd gotten the hell out of there.

Progressing steadily toward the two willows, a crocodile moved silently next to the boat . . . maybe four feet away. It was obviously watching with intense interest, its head slightly breaking the surface and hardly noticeable except for the eyes. Feeling fairly safe in the boat, Hans continued on. While minding to his own business, he hoped the crocodile would do the same. With a sinister smile, he wondered if perhaps the croc viewed him as his business. It also crossed his mind the crocodile might be hoping the human was bringing him another meal.

Approaching the exact spot and not needing to delve further into the murky water, he was relieved to find her still there. Although not certain how much of her was present, her nightgown—browning and in shreds—was still entangled under the water.

Feeling liberated, he could finally set the silly imagined sightings aside and concentrate on leaving for new clothes and much needed boots.

Paddling out of the marsh grass and clear of the swamp, Hans thought he saw a boat docked at the landing and maybe two figures standing near it. If one of them happened to be Mr. Wayland, how could he explain his whereabouts? Thinking it best to stay out of sight and paddle farther down river . . . but not too far, he'd keep out of the current and close to the riverbank. It would mean a longer walk back to his horse but a safer outcome without questions. As he moved along and examined the riverbank, he saw a clear spot with no obvious crocs sunning themselves.

Stepping cautiously out of boat and looking for something substantial to tie the boat to, he glanced back at the water, wanting to make sure no croc had followed him onto the bank. Out of his side vision, a large black snake appeared, rippling through the water's surface and seemingly swimming directly at him. When he stepped back to get a better footing on drier land, he stepped on what he thought was a tree branch. Feeling it move and taking another look, he'd stepped on another snake. It immediately coiled and aggressively sprung toward him with a flash of whiteness in its open mouth. Losing his balance, it latched into him. It was at least five feet long; and for a spit second, they were eye to eye. Falling, he tried to pull it from his neck; but it wouldn't let go. Tugging at it and attempting to get upright, he slipped into a wet dip in the ground, realizing he'd fallen into a squirming litter of young cottonmouths. Screaming in fright and pain, he tried to crawl away but to no avail. Bitten at least fifteen or so times, the last thing he heard before dying was the sound of a loud rooster's crow nearby.

When the workers stopped for lunch at the usual time, it was odd the overseer was not there to tell them what to do in the afternoon. Finishing their customary rushed lunch break, they looked at each other with wide-opened eyes and confusion. Should they continue with their morning tasks, should they wait to receive new directions, or should they return to their cabins? After another hour passed, some workers returned to their previous assignments while others wandered about aimlessly. No one seemed to want to venture back to their cabin, fearing they would be in serious trouble.

Jefferson—who never sought another's opinion and liked being a loner—considered himself smarter than the others. Looking about for someone to speak up, he finally said to no one in particular, "This no good. Boss always here bout time for eats. Best goes to see if he be hurt or in troubles." Many of the workers stared in his direction while others shook their heads in disbelief . . . as if to silently say, it wouldn't be a good idea.

It took him sometime to walk from the field back to the overseer's cabin. After knocking several times with no answer, he left to look in the stable. Not finding his horse there, Jefferson was perplexed as to what to do next. Perhaps Boss left and didn't tell no one and then gots hurt. If that was the case, the Master would not be mad at him for leaving the field.

Although afraid to approach the main house, if he could help the overseer, perhaps it would be a good reason to get moved into a better working spot.

With his knees banging together, Jefferson knocked on the backdoor and waited for a house helper to answer. With no response after a second knocking, he slowly turned to leave. He guessed he'd go back and wait with the others. If the overseer was there, he'd try to sneak back without being noticed.

Sallie, the new kitchen helper, opened the door and said, "Boy, what youse doin' here?"

Answered back quickly, "I's lookin' for Boss Man."

"Youse be gettin' on your way. Massa don't talk to the likes of youse."

"I's lookin' for the other boss."

"Is youse thick in the head? He not here; he be with the workers out yonder," Sallie answered, pointing toward the fields.

Almost defiantly, Jefferson answered, "No, he ain't. Wees don't know what to doos."

"I gots work to do . . . can't bees talkin' to youse no more."

Calling from somewhere behind Sallie, Abigail's voice was heard. "Sallie, we're waiting for our tea. Quit your lollygagging."

Turning away from Jefferson, Sallie answered, "Sorry Mistress. I doos it right aways."

Shutting the door in Jefferson's face, Sallie ran for the teapot. Placing it on the already prepared tray, she hurried to the dining room.

Waiting for Sallie to finish serving them, Abigail said, "Sallie, I know you are new to your duties but don't be talking to the outside workers. They are below your station as a household helper. If you like staying in the outside kitchen and want to continue working inside the house, then you mustn't talk to an outside worker during the hours you are serving Master and myself. Do you understand?"

"Yes, Mistress."

"And what did he want to talk about?" Abigail inquired.

"I's sorry, Mistress."

Dismissing her with a flip of the wrist, Abigail asked again, "What did he talk to you about?"

Sallie answered but continued to look down at the floor, "He lookin' for his work boss." Hearing the words 'work boss,' William suddenly took notice of their conversation.

Looking in Sallie's direction, William asked, "What did you just say?"

"I's sorry Massa. I no talk to hims again."

"I understand Sallie. Was he looking for the overseer?"

With her head still lowered, she answered, "I's reckons so."

Pushing his chair back and standing, William said, "Abigail, there must be a problem. I will be back directly as soon as I sort this out. We will continue our conversation about Teresa Anne when I return."

# Chapter 11

William left the manor in a sprint, hoping to encounter the worker behind the building but did not see him or anyone else on his way to the overseer's cabin. Knocking and calling out to Hans, he opened the cabin door, thinking he might be inside but unable to answer. It didn't take long to peruse the single room or its meager furnishings. Walking quickly to the fireplace—to feel for warmth—he found the bricks cold to the touch.

Not locating Hans at his first stop, William set out for the stable. From there, he'd continue on to the fields. As William looked for Hans, he wasn't sure if he was concerned, angry, or perplexed about his being gone. It was beyond his understanding for this to be happening. Why was Hans not attending to his duties . . . even worse, leaving the workers unsupervised? Surely, he wouldn't just up and leave without permission. There had to be a reasonable answer to this dilemma, he mused.

Entering the stable, it dawned on him . . . no one was there to saddle his horse. Disgusted, he would need to do it himself. While gathering items to saddle his horse, he walked by the stall where the overseer kept his horse, noticing the board to keep the animal in was down and the horse missing. Well, at least now he knew

Hans was riding his horse . . . but where? Perhaps, he'd fallen, was injured, and out of ear-shot. William shuddered as he recalled Ronald's fall.

It seemed to take a lengthy amount of time to bridle his horse, throw the saddle over the blanket, and cinch the girth. He tried to remember the last time he'd saddled a horse but couldn't. No longer a young man, he was breathing hard and puffing when he finished. Double checking to make sure the saddle was cinched tightly and wouldn't slide down when he stepped into the stirrup, he mounted the horse with a bit of personal satisfaction.

Riding toward the fields, he sought out the field with the most workers clustered in one place. When he saw them, he loosened the reigns and slapped his horse to go faster. Once close enough to talk without hollering, he pulled his horse up and asked, "When was the overseer here last?"

The workers looked at him with surprise, but no one answered. "Listen up, I want to know when you saw your boss last. Gather closer together and hurry up about it," William demanded. Giving them a moment to follower his orders, he yelled at a few stragglers digging around nearby cotton plants. "You . . . over there, get with the others."

Taking in a deep breath, he asked, "Does anyone know where the overseer is?" Again, he received no response to his question. A few of the workers shook their heads back and forth to his inquiry, but most stood quietly with bowed heads. Exasperated, he looked through the workers before asking, "Where is Jefferson?"

"Here, Boss," Jefferson answered, stepping from the center of the group to the front.

"Jefferson, did you come to the house earlier . . . to the back entrance?"

Hesitantly, Jefferson answered with a question, "Did I do wrong?"

"No, no. Can you tell me when your boss was last here? And did he say when he'd be back?"

"No, Massa. He goes from field to field early but always back for eatin' time. We waitin' for knowin' what to doos after eatin'."

Looking at the group of twenty or so men, women, and children, William said, "You can all go back to your cabins and wait for further instructions . . . except for you, Jefferson."

Jefferson looked straight ahead, fearing he was singled out for punishment. Remaining still, he watched the others leave out of the corners of his eyes. Expecting the worst, he calmly waited for Massa's horse to come in his direction and stop.

Once beside Jefferson, William said, "I'll direct those with mules to unhitch them and take them back to the barn. You are to keep one mule here to ride. Start looking for the overseer. Look from the big house to the river. I've already looked in the barn and stable. While you're looking yonder, I will search the other fields. Do you understand?"

Answered with relief, Jefferson said, "Yes, Massa."

Proud to be selected by Massa to help in the search, Jefferson was determined to find the overseer. He started behind the main building, passing the outside kitchen, the smoke house, the wash house, the chicken house and connected pen, until finally searching around the pig pens. From there he looked into the worker's graveyard before crossing into the willow tree area. While raising his arms to keep the low hanging branches from slapping against his face, it was difficult to direct the mule. Sometimes the animal traveled in circles and seemed to purposely seek out the lowest branches—almost as if he wanted to knock him off—and refused to cooperate. Finally arriving at the clearing created by the barn's charred remains, he didn't see anyone or anything suspicious. Beginning to have doubts of finding the overseer, he dejectedly left to search by the river. His first stop would be the boat dock. He was familiar with that part of the plantation, having loaded and unloaded supplies there many times.

Seeing the overseer's horse, Jefferson called out, "Boss, where you be?" Jumping off the mule, he took notice of the surroundings before stepping onto the landing. As he walked back and forth on the wooden planks, he stopped a few times to gaze into the water. He even bent over both ends of the dock to peer underneath. Calling out several times, it did cross his mind the overseer might have gone into the water to wash himself and been taken away by a hungry croc. Best to find Massa and let him knows the horse was at the dock. Should he take the horse back with him or leave it be? Deciding, it was best not take it without permission.

Leaving the dock, the mule moved along briskly until approaching the barn. Balking near the building's entrance, it refused to move beyond the barn. Cussing under his breath, Jefferson whipped and kicked it several times but received no forward progress. As a last resort, he jumped off and slowly pushed, pulled, and tugged it onward. Once, out of sight of the barn, the mule started to walk, enabling Jefferson to jump back on and ride it in the direction of the fields. Almost to the nearest field, he saw Massa coming; his horse lathered and breathing hard.

Once within speaking distance, Jefferson said, "I finds his horse by the river."

"But not the overseer," William inquired like a statement. Before Jefferson could answer, William quickly asked, "Did the horse look like he'd been in the water?"

"No, Massa."

"Was the horse injured . . . ah, hurt?"

"No, Massa. He be tied at the dock."

"Hmm," was William's thoughtful reply. "Good job. I will take it from here."

Watching the Massa hurry off in the direction of the river, Jefferson was left wondering what to do next. He reckoned he'd put the mule back in the barn and return to his cabin. This time, it was easy to guide the animal to its resting place; it eagerly cooperated without being prodded.

William approached the landing, looking cautiously for clues to the overseer's whereabouts. At the end of the landing were several fifty pound bags of rice and grain stacked three high. Those supplies were supposed to be delivered tomorrow, he thought with annoyance. Perhaps there was a problem between the men who brought the supplies and Hans. With no sign of his overseer . . . yet his horse was there; he could make no sense of it. First Kizzi disappeared and now Hans. Walking back to mount his horse, something wasn't right; he just couldn't lay a finger on it. Halfway back to the manor, it hit him. Was the fishing boat tied to the dock? He couldn't remember if he saw it or not. Disgusted with himself for not paying better attention, he returned to look. No, it was missing.

Although more confused than ever, it seemed to make sense that if the horse was tied by the landing and the boat gone, then Hans must have left in the boat. That assumption created a new question . . . why? Well, if and when Hans returned, he'd not find his horse waiting. And he better have a good reason for this puzzlement. If not and regardless of how much he depended on him, he'd send him packing.

In order to get through the remainder of the day, there was much for him to do. What ought to be done depended on how much the workers did routinely and how much they were told to do each day by the overseer. He would gather the workers together again to learn who did what.

Perhaps Jefferson could help sort out the arrangements of who handled which chores: such as moving the supplies from the landing to storage, taking care of the evening animal feedings, and who milked the cows. Hans had previously talked about Jefferson in positive terms, and he'd been impressed with his taking the initiative to come to the house for help. The fact he'd followed his orders today was impressive . . . even locating the overseer's horse.

Damn, it had been years since he'd had hands-on interaction with the workers, and he didn't look forward to dealing with them again. Before Hans arrived, he'd had two overseers directing the day to day operations of the plantation. When Hans took over the position, he'd been able to do a better job all by himself. Little by little, he'd allowed Hans to take care of the fields and the workers without interference from him. Hans had enabled him to concentrate on finances, becoming involved only when a problem arose. Why had Hans done this to him?

If Hans was still gone tomorrow, or if he never returned; the need to seek out a new overseer as soon as possible would become his most important priority. He knew full well it would be physically impossible to undertake the task on his own. He would not kid himself; the truth of the matter . . . he was too old to even try.

# Chapter 12

*H*ungry and frustrated, William sluggishly entered the manor. Feeling it pointless to look for Abigail on the main floor, he wearily climbed the stairs and entered her room. Expecting to find her sleeping, he was surprised when she wasn't in bed. Perplexed and turning to leave, he was startled to see her lying in a huddled position in the farthest corner. His first reaction . . . now what? When he called her name, she neither answered nor moved.

While cautiously approaching and standing above her, he hesitantly asked, "Abigail, what are you doing there?"

When she neither moved nor responded, he worriedly placed a hand on her shoulder and gently tried to rouse her. As if confronted by wild animals, she screamed, shot upward from the floor, and flailed her arms in all directions.

Jerking backward and almost falling, he hollered, "It's William."

"Tell her to leave me be," Abigail shrieked.

"Abigail, it's William," he repeated. "Calm yourself. You've had a terrible nightmare and walked in your sleep. Why in heaven's name are you on the floor?" he quizzed. Beyond his comprehension and not expecting a sane answer, he added, "It's the damn potion making you act crazy in the head."

"William, please don't fuss at me. Can't you see I'm frightened?"

"Of what? What is frightening you?"

"I get no peace. She follows me," Abigail answered; her whole body shaking uncontrollably.

"Who's following you?" he asked, trying his best to understand her plight.

"You don't understand; she won't let anyone else see her."

"My dear, it's the opium that makes you imagine these things. Have you had any food today?" Not waiting for an answer, he continued, "Come with me and we'll have some nourishment together. Everything will appear better after you've eaten."

"I'm not hungry. Food sounds awful," she finally replied.

Realizing he'd also not eaten since daybreak, William truthfully countered, "Well, I am famished; food sounds wonderful."

Placing his arm around Abigail's waist, he suddenly realized how frail she'd become. He wouldn't bother to discuss his new problem created by the overseer's disappearance or mention Theresa Anne's baby coming early and being puny. Under these circumstances, it seemed more helpful to have a conversation about her getting better.

While holding onto Abigail's arm and helping her down the stairs, he reminded himself to look for her opium hiding place. No, the search would need to wait until later. As soon as he had food in his stomach, he needed to talk to Jefferson and the other workers before it was too late. The sun would soon be setting.

Quickly gulping down his sweet tea and hardly chewing his vittles of sow belly and collard greens, he watched Abigail move her food slowly back and forth across her plate. "Abigail, please eat something. At least have a slice of cornbread. Do you want me to have Sallie prepare something more to your liking?"

With fluttering eyes, she mumbled, "Not hungry." Immediately after responding, she placed her head on the table beside her plate and closed her eyes.

"Abigail, what would your children say if they saw you at this moment?"

"I'm safe now," she finally answered. "She won't come while you're here."

Frustrated, he replied, "That's utter nonsense. You are making me angry. You must eat. Besides, I can't stay by your side every minute. There are outside problems to attend to."

With tightly closed eyes and twitching shoulders, she whispered, "Don't leave me. She's lurking just out of sight."

"If I have Bessie come sit with you, will you eat then?"

"I'm tired . . . so tired. Will you help me to bed. I just need to rest. If you won't stay with me, would you ask Sallie to sit by my bed until you return?"

"Of course, my dear." But as he answered, he was already planning to help her upstairs and watch where she kept the opium. He wasn't sure what would happen when he snatched it away, but he'd soon find out. She could not continue in this state; something had to be done for her sake and his.

Watching Abigail until she seemed somewhat comfortable, he didn't mention the potion and surprisingly, she didn't seem to be hankering for it. Standing next to the bed, he waited a moment before asking, "Is there anything you wish before I leave?"

"Yes, would you hurry to fetch Sallie and stay with me until she comes?"

Confused, tired and not understanding how he could both leave and stay, it seemed hopeless to question her request. Why Sallie instead of Bessie, he wondered. Knowing she'd get all riled up if he didn't promptly locate Sallie, he hastily left. Stepping into the hall, he paused to listen, but all seemed quiet within. But just in case she left the bed to retrieve the opium; he waited another minute or so before peeking inside . . . but nothing had changed.

William found Sallie where she belonged . . . in the kitchen fixin' pig intestines. Feeling himself frown, he didn't like telling her to stop what she was doing, especially since she was preparing his favorite food. He'd not enjoyed chitlins since before Matilda's passing. Bessie would have been a better choice, he mused.

Sallie seemed puzzled when told to sit with the mistress until he came back but said nothing nor asked any questions. Noticing her demeanor, he added, "She is feeling poorly and would like you to be close-by her bedside. I have things to do before it gets dark. It should not be long before I return."

Leaving the house, William reflected on why Sallie instead of Bessie. Since Matilda asked for Sallie to come inside first, perhaps that was why she wanted her instead of Bessie. At this point it was beyond his reasoning to question how or why Abigail thought about anything.

Going directly to the worker cabins, he remembered where he'd seen Jefferson earlier so started with that cabin first. Only knocking once, Jefferson appeared immediately, saying, "I's here Massa."

"Jefferson, have everyone come out. I need to talk to them."

Jefferson rushed to each of the cabin doors while calling, "Come outside . . . Massa wants to see youse."

When assembled, William began. "The overseer is gone. I need to know who does what, so the plantation doesn't suffer until I can hire a new overseer. It is still my hope Hans will return by the morrow. Should this not come to pass, I need everyone's attention to the matters at hand. Let's start with the feeding of the livestock."

William was surprised to learn that each worked according to his or her daily assignments . . . doled out in advance by the overseer. He was reassured to learn that those responsible for the animals had already cared for them. His second surprise was learning the workers' different tasks were accomplished each day without prodding. They went about their business on their own unless a problem arose. The only questions not covered were about the day to day care of the cotton fields. Inquiring further, he was told Hans rang a bell every morning to make sure the workers were assembled and ready to toil in the fields according to his directions for the day.

Somewhat relieved, he'd look for the bell in the overseer's cabin and ring it at daybreak. He asked Jefferson to stay with him until the others returned to their cabins.

"Jefferson, If you are able, I need your assistance in answering some general questions. Have the workers received their allotment of food for the month?"

His answer was clear and direct. "All but rice. I'm thinkin' the bags left on the dock might be rice."

"Tell some of the men—you choose which ones—to help place the bags in storage. Tell them I said so," William added forcibly. "Also, if you hear anything about the whereabouts of the overseer, I'd surely like to know. Do you understand?"

With a nod and, "Yes Massa," from Jefferson, William sighed and turned away.

Not gone from Abigail for as long as expected, William walked slowly into the manor but did not go directly to her room. Instead, he went into the library and poured himself a whisky. He did not sip it for enjoyment but rather downed it in one gulp.

Pouring another whiskey—this time, at least two fingers high—William sat down and reflected on how the duties of an overseer had changed since the war and commencement of recon-struction. Amazed at how organized Hans had been, he was still perplexed by his leaving. After giving the meeting with the work-ers more thoughtful consideration, he'd again give Hans the benefit of having a good reason for leaving before seeking a replacement. Depressed, he thought how wonderful it would be to have sons to help at times like this, but sadly, it wasn't to be.

Thinking about what needed to be done on the plantation in the interim, the workers were doing the same tasks as they did back in slavery days. But now it was important to keep them reasonably happy while getting the most production from them without the accompanied punishment. If a worker became unhappy with his or her situation or perhaps thought they were pushed too hard, they'd simply vanish during the night and not show up for work the next day. Since no longer a possession—and what made the situation even worse—when a worker disappeared, there was no use searching for him. And, if happened upon, a plantation owner's only choice was whether or not to allow the worker to come back. Punishment or discipline was no longer an option.

During the years of slave labor, he'd basically ignored the overseer's actions pertaining to worker discipline. Seldom did he take part or even watch when the slaves were routinely tied to the whipping post and beaten in the old barn. Not that it was repugnant to him; his priority was doing what was necessary in order to make a profit. During those times, it was a known fact that punishment kept the workers under control and productive, so letting the overseer handle the day to day discipline wasn't his concern.

After the war and slave freedom, a few workers showed an air of independence . . . even holding their heads up when spoken to. He'd gradually become accustomed to it, so it bothered him less and less as time went by. At that juncture all he could do was accept it as a sign of the times. Progress it was called.

A few former slave workers—the ones still living on the plantation since the war—were mostly too old to look for work elsewhere. Naturally, they no longer pulled their own weight, but the others were protective of them . . . watching to make sure they were treated fairly while doing menial tasks.

The plantation overseers—now considered supervisors—were still responsible for the care of livestock, the agricultural implements, and cotton production but needed to have these tasks accomplished without the previous day-to-day cruelty. The supervisors were also responsible to see the workers were fed and given materials to make their own clothing in a fair and just manner. It had become standard practice to give an additional food allotment or a better work position as a reward rather than using punishment. Shaking his head, all this and he still paid them too, he thought.

Hans had done a terrific job and although difficult to admit, there was no way he could step in and run the plantation even close to his success. Damn it, expecting his best crop in years—even better than last year's—and now this. Instinctively aware of his own limitations, if Hans didn't return, he'd need to rely on his own experience, and the prospect of that didn't sit well. It was his hope-ful prayer he could survive until either Hans returned or another overseer was found. Since good overseers were in high demand, it crossed his mind Hans could have sought out other employment with more pay and been too cowardly to tell him. Hans did say he needed time off for a few days.

When William warily climbed the stairs to check on Abigail, it dawned on him . . . he'd forgotten to look for the bell to ring at sun-rise. Damn, he was already tired and the worst was yet to come. Turning, he left the house just as the sun was setting. Almost to the cabin, he realized it would be impossible to see inside without a lamp. Returning to the manor, he chastised himself even more. How could he run the plantation when he couldn't think two steps ahead of himself?

Back again, he guardedly entered the overseer's cabin, feel-ing he'd intruded into another's domain without invitation. Considering most everything he saw or touched belonged to him, it was an odd sensation. On the table he found an oil lamp next to a large brass bell. While contemplating on what else he might need and not wanting to come there again, he carefully looked around. Satisfied, he closed the door quietly behind him. He couldn't help but wonder why a white man would live such an isolated and meager existence with next to nothing—no family and only meager possessions. Not of interest to him before and certainly not of interest to him now, he was intolerably angry with Hans for placing him in this dire situation.

Today, he would be having his fourth interview for the position of overseer . . . the fourth within two weeks. The person he was waiting to talk to had been recommended by the seed provider in Vicksburg and was supposedly knowledgeable in cotton production. Because he would be the first man of color to seek the position, William had little or no confidence he'd work out. However, because of the necessity to get the cotton picked and delivered to the mill—a must to clear his numerous debts—he was bordering on desperate.

A considerable part of his desperation also involved Abigail. She had continued with her strange and anxious moods, often rushing about without a particular destination—her eyes darting sporadically to the side and sometimes stopping to look behind her. Sometimes, she babbled to the point of being so child-like he feared she'd completely lost her senses. He'd written to Teresa Anne . . . asking her to come home and help with her mother, but the replied correspondence said she was unable to do so . . . stating poor heath since giving birth. Her words were apologetic, explaining her weakness to do even the smallest of tasks. Finishing her letter, he felt sorry for her plight and for a brief moment did not think of his own troubles. His only sensible answer was to pull two women from the outside to watch over Abigail until he returned at the end of each day. And even though she now had additional help, Abigail was still unable to function normally or instruct the day-to-day operations of the manor. Each frustrating day endured—whether inside or out—was long and tiring with little rest at night. Sometimes, he was so tuckered-out and weary; he slept in his dirty clothing and didn't care.

While he nervously waited in the parlor to interview yet another possible overseer, his mind wandered back to the previous night when awakened by Abigail's yelling. Thinking she was in danger, he'd rushed into her room, finding her standing at the window. Not sure if she was talking to him or not, she'd said, "There she goes. See her . . . see her."

"See who?" he'd asked.

Watching intently out the window, she'd answered matter-of-factly, "Kizzi."

"Step away from the window, so I can look," he'd replied. As he walked toward the window, he would have been more interested if this same scenario had not happened numerous times before . . . always at night when he was exhausted from work and lack of sleep.

"My dear, all is quiet below. We've been about this before. Kizzi is never coming back. Remember, you said she was gone . . . and good riddance to her . . . you'd said."

"You don't understand. She won't harm her own blood. She told me so."

"Abigail, this is craziness. Come with me and go back to bed."

"William, if you love me you'll stay by my side and protect me."

"Have you forgotten . . . Hans is gone and there is no one to help me supervise getting the cotton delivered to the mill? Jefferson helps as best he can but has little cotton expertise. I must get some rest in order to carry on."

As if she didn't hear his words or heard them and didn't care, Abigail yelled, "My father said you were worthless and just after his money. I know you bedded Kizzi's mother and no telling how many others. Get out of here."

Ignoring her callous statements—although truthful—William asked, "Abigail, might your medicine help to calm you?"

"It's all gone," she hollered back. Then just as quickly, her demeanor changed and she sweetly added, "Perhaps you could procure more from the doctor. Not that it does any good."

Before he had a chance to answer, she yelled again and even louder, "Get out of my sight this minute."

As he'd left her bedroom last night, he'd promised himself that after the overseer's interview, he'd somehow acquire more opium . . . if not for Abigail's rest but for his own. It couldn't possibly make her any worse than she already was.

# *Chapter 13*

*B*essie entered the parlor, saying, "He follows me and won't stay 'til I's fetch you. I's sorry."

"It's alright, Bessie. Shut the door when you leave," William answered calmly.

Almost proudly, the person in front of him stated, "My name in Benjamin. I was told you are looking for a crop manager."

"Yes, my overseer left quite suddenly. It's almost harvest time and much to do in order to get the crop to the mill. Tell me what experience you have in such matters."

Learning of Benjamin's decision to come south because the fields to the north were inundated with workers and supervisors; he was quick to mention how wages had dropped dramatically for qualified persons such as himself. He was seeking a position with better pay . . . assuring William several times of his qualifications and would do his utmost to get the job done properly and in a timely manner.

"That sounds reasonable, but how do I know you can stand behind your words?"

"Sir, I am an educated man, and you can trust my word. If I displease you, you can tell me to leave with no hard-feelings. May I ask who has been doing the management to this point?"

"I have been doing most of it with the help of a worker named Jefferson."

Benjamin then stated forwardly, "Before you decide, I have questions of you. I would like to bring my family down from the north in due time . . . that is to say if you are satisfied with my work. I don't work on Sunday unless there is an emergency. I am a Christian man and keep Sunday for church and prayer. I would like your present helper, ah . . . Jefferson, to assist me unless he has a problem with doing so. And if he's not to my liking, then I want your permission to choose someone else among your workers to assist me."

After further intense inquiries into Benjamin's experience, William asked, "Does six hundred dollars per year, plus a place for you and your family to stay, and a spot to grow your own vegetables sound acceptable?"

"I'm thinking I would be happier with seven hundred plus the other considerations."

They looked at each other eye-to-eye before William answered, "Done."

"One final thing," Benjamin added, "I don't hanker on cruelty but rather abide by a contented worker treated fairly as a more productive worker. I have heard you are also such a man."

"Would you like a signed contract?" William asked.

"I would rather shake your hand . . . man-to-man," Benjamin answered, looking William in the eye again.

"Then, it's a done deal," William answered before offering his hand. Let's walk out to the overseer's cabin.

As they walked, William could not remember offering his hand to a man of color before. Times had definitely changed. Was his desperate situation making it an easier choice or was his nature softening. Either way, he prayed Benjamin would do a good job for him.

When they entered the cabin, Benjamin had a confused . . . almost repugnant look on his face. After glancing around the room several times, he asked, "Am I to understand your overseer lived here with his family?"

"No, he was a single man," William replied.

"Sir, with all due respect I could not have my wife and two children live in one room. Perhaps there is another larger cabin?"

Thinking quickly, William responded, "No, but if you are handy and with the help of others, you can open an entrance into the adjoining cabin to enlarge your living quarters. I have no problem with that. I can only ask you to first concentrate on the cotton picking so as not to take the workers away from their important tasks."

"I hear and understand your concern. Where should I put my horse and where do I find Jefferson?"

"I will find Jefferson and have him take care of your horse." William answered.

"Sir, again with all due respect, I can handle the horse myself. Perhaps we can find Jefferson together? Then, Jefferson can return with me to where my horse will be housed, giving us a chance to talk. Would this be acceptable to you?"

"An even better choice," William answered.

A mere hour later and after telling Benjamin and Jefferson he could be reached in the manor, William returned to the parlor and sighed. He was happy to have made a decision and better yet, it seemed like the right one. Only time would tell if it was the best one. Worn out yet relieved, he rested his head against the back of the sofa and quickly dosed off.

# Chapter 14

Although constantly worried about the upcoming cotton harvest, William realized the months had gone by quickly. Everyone associated with the plantation had been exceedingly busy in one way or another. Even the weather cooperated with the growing season and harvest. Benjamin turned out to be a life saver in many ways, and their relationship progressed into a mutual respect for each other's position. He'd gradually grown to appreciate Benjamin's cotton knowledge and now relied on—even trusted—his decision making. Unable to openly share these thoughts with his new supervisor, he was careful to appear standoffish at all times. To do otherwise would be against tradition and his upbringing.

Not certain how Benjamin acquired additional field workers to cultivate and pick the cotton, but this year's yield proved to be the best ever. Even the atmosphere throughout the plantation felt different from previous years. Everyone seemed happier . . . regularly singing and playing music at the end of each exhausting day. Benjamin initiated ringing a bell at lunch time—giving them more time to eat and rest, set up more drinking stations—allowing them to stop and drink without asking permission, and as long as they continued to work, they were permitted to talk and sing. It never failed to amaze him by the amount of work accomplished with fewer rules. Unlike the days under Hans, the pickers moved across the fields in parallel lines . . . talking, laughing, and singing. If not witnessed by his own eyes, he wouldn't have believed it. With his blessings the overseer's cabin had been enlarged, and Benjamin would soon be traveling north to assist with his family's move to the plantation . . . wanting them to be settled in before time to plant next year's crop.

With time William accepted the loss of his three sons as a part of life's cruel trials and tribulations. While eventually coming to grips with his misfortune, he was able to acknowledge his loss was not unlike others who'd lost children to illness or sons to that horrible war. Although accepting his fate in life, he was still angered by the devastation of lives, limbs, and property left behind. Often noting—during heated conversations with others—how nothing could be done to make any of it right again . . . ever, ever, ever.

His life had become somewhat calm again . . . except for Abigail's declining mental and physical health. Receiving around the clock attention from the household staff, she seldom left her bed or bedroom. Following the worst of times, especially when her behavior was so bizarre she became uncontrollable, he'd finally procured more opium. The potion kept her less combative, sleeping most of the time, and quiet when awake. Her imaginary sightings had all but ceased except for an occasional, "There she goes." Although living under the same roof, he seldom saw his wife . . . scarcely able to lay eyes on her without cringing or dashing away in disgust.

Soon, he'd be traveling to Vicksburg to purchase seed, and since his daughter's health was fully improved, she was coming to look after Abigail while he was away. When posting his request to Teresa Anne, he'd been less than forthright in discussing her mother's condition, preferring to tell her in person when she arrived.

After the recent successful and profitable harvest, William was actually looking forward to getting away to buy seed, collect miscellaneous provisions, and stock up on good whiskey. If all went according to his expectations, perhaps there would be time for suitable and purposeful conversation with other landowners.

He'd heard through the grape-vine that people were getting sick in and around Vicksburg . . . even dying from a strange sickness which turned their skin yellow. Planning on being there for a mere two or three days at the most—just enough time to gather the items on his wish list, purchase seed, and set up transportation—he wasn't concerned. He didn't plan on associating with anyone who appeared ill, feeling confident he wouldn't be placing himself in harm's way. Since most of the cotton seed for this part of Mississippi was purchased in Vicksburg, it was more than likely the rumors were over-blown to keep seed prices high.

His fishing boat had recently been found ten miles downriver, snagged within overhanging branches and not noticed for months. Luckily, his last name and those of his boys had been carved into the bench plank and recognized by the finder. By the time he'd learned of the boat's return, the person had already left. He was disappointed for the inability to do the proper thing of personally thanking the person and giving him a small token of appreciation for his honesty. Even more so, he'd lost the opportunity to ask additional questions. However, Benjamin assured him the man was in a hurry and only wanted to return the boat to its rightful owner. Quoting the man's exact words, "It's as I found it a week past . . . not damaged and has both oars present on the bottom. I know nothing more than that." William eventually concluded the boat became unfettered from the dock and drifted off . . . having nothing to do with Hans. It would always remain a mystery why Hans would up and leave without a word, but he'd gotten past it . . . hesitantly moving on. Nevertheless and with Benjamin's assistance, it soon became easier to stop questioning why, especially since the plantation was running smoothly again. More importantly and with enormous relief, the cotton money had been received and distributed to his creditors.

Teresa Anne arrived the day before her father was scheduled to leave. As soon as the carriage came to a full stop, she jumped out and rushed halfway up the front steps to meet him. Throwing her arms around him, she giddily said, "Hi Daddy. Is Mama in her room?"

Flabbergasted by the way she'd bolted so quickly to him and without the appropriate decorum, he nodded, followed by answering, "We need to talk."

"We will," she flippantly replied before hustling into the house.

He'd wanted to warn Teresa Anne first. In his mind she would join him in the parlor for a heart-to-heart, and he'd prepare her prior to seeing her mother. Since there was no way to overtake

Teresa Anne before she reached Abigail's room, he pointed toward Bessie and the others assembled beside her, "Fetch her possessions and take them inside."

Ignoring the household workers as they hurried past him, William stepped toward the manor. Thinking he'd forgotten something, he stopped and glanced back, seeing a statuesque woman of color standing beside the carriage and holding Teresa Anne's child. Casting a second and more scrutinizing look, he was immediately drawn to her face. She possessed the same natural elegance and facial characteristics as Kizzi's mother. The resemblance was uncanny—the high cheek bones and round eyes. She stood there with sheer simplicity, yet a powerful all-knowing aloofness surrounded her. In a flash of remembrance, his knees wobbled, and he gulped.

He didn't want to walk in her direction or take the child from her. But oddly uncomfortable, he didn't want to ignore her either and leave. So, he motioned for her to come toward him. As she grew closer, it was all he could do not to stare deeply into her eyes. Within a few feet, he said in a stern voice, "Follow me. Do not drop the child as you climb the steps."

Hoping he sounded forceful and the person in charge, he waited for her response. Never lowering her gaze, she did not speak but rather responded with a slight dip of her head. Repositioning the child on her hip, she appeared to be waiting until he started to proceed up the steps. As they moved upward, he could feel her presence closely behind. Just before he reached the front door, she began to hum softly and whisper soothing yet indecipherable words.

Once within the entrance hallway, William hesitated before turning in the servant's direction and saying, "Stay with the child until his mother returns." Looking at the child, he found it interesting to see the once whimpering baby had fallen fast asleep in just a matter of minutes. Glancing around, he observed Bessie and the others standing among a multitude of bags and traveling trunks, causing him to wonder how long Teresa Anne planned on staying.

"Bessie, you and the others take Teresa Anne's possessions to the room prepared for her."

On his way to Abigail's room, William thought how the house was bursting with helpers—scurrying about in a similar manner to the way they did before the war—but sadly, most were now there mainly to assist with Abigail. Sighing, he imagined the joy Abigail would derive from telling them what to do and freely barking orders at them like an overseer.

When William reached Abigail's room, the door was closed; his wife's attendant standing outside and fidgeting. Reaching for the door knob, the door abruptly opened. Face-to-face with Teresa Anne, her ashen complexion and watery eyes—full of bewilderment—looked directly back at him. "Oh my dear, I wanted to warn you. Let's go downstairs and talk." Taking her hand, William motioned to Abigail's attendant to return to his wife's side.

As they walked toward the parlor, William sought to move the conversation momentarily away from Abigail, so he paused and remarked, "I'm embarrassed to inquire, but I've forgotten your son's name."

With tears streaming quietly down her cheeks, a cracking voice replied, "His given name is Ethan William . . . after his two grandfathers."

Walking again, William continued, "That was kind of you; I'm delighted by your choice." After an uncomfortable silence, he stated, "I've had the bedroom across the hall from your mother's prepared for your stay. Also, a small bed was placed there; the mattress cautioned for bed bugs." Not wanting to delve into the problems with Abigail any sooner than necessary, he said, "I should have, but didn't, consider you were bringing your servant along." Taking a deep breath, he continued, "I hope the accommodations are to your liking. Your mother always handled such things." Noticing his voice beginning to quiver, he cleared his throat and swallowed before speaking again. "The household workers will assist you in any way you desire. They have been instructed to do your bidding as if I personally directed them myself."

Just before entering the parlor, William lowered his eyes and asked, "What is the child's servant's name . . . in case I need to address her?"

"Her name is Melanie. Daddy, she is just wonderful. She has been nothing but kind to our family during my long illness and recovery. Ethan adores her."

"I'm sure Bessie can locate an appropriate room for her, fairly close to yours. You can make your wishes known to Bessie. I'm no longer familiar with who stays where and truthfully . . . I don't care." Not wanting to appear interested in where Teresa Anne's servant was placed, he decided to change the subject. But sheepishly, he was most curious . . . nay, more interested in the child's servant than the child.

Barely inside the parlor, a more composed Teresa Anne initiated a flurry of questions. "What's happened to Mama? Why the boils on her arms? She hardly knows me, slurring her words and not making the slightest bit of sense. I had no idea. It's terrible . . . just terrible. Is this because of Ronald's death?"

Remaining quiet until closing the door, William replied, "Teresa Anne, could we sit a spell?" Waiting until she seemed comfortable on the sofa, her hands clasped tightly around the handkerchief in her lap, he said, "I wish I knew the answer. I cannot make heads or tails of it. She is taking a potion to keep her quiet. Otherwise, she runs through the house . . . trying to hide."

"Hiding from what?" Teresa Anne asked, trying to understand her father's perplexing statements.

"It seems she no longer knows what's real or imagined. I'm sorry you must see her like this, but I must go to Vicksburg to purchase seed before planting time passes. I didn't know what else to do." No longer able to keep his emotions in check William's voice faltered, and he began to cry. "I'm embarrassed beyond words. A father is supposed to be strong for his children. I should be able to control myself, but I'm tired of pretending that all is well when it isn't. Teresa Anne, please forgive my weakness. I am terribly sorry for my behavior."

"Daddy, I'm the one who's sorry. Why didn't you tell me?"

"I was afraid you wouldn't come," William answered truthfully.

"I want to help but don't understand any of this. Tell me what to do while you're away?"

As they discussed incidentals—like who did what and such—their conversation was interrupted by loud crying from outside the parlor's door.

"Oh my goodness, I need to nurse my baby and then settle in. Once he's back to sleep, can we talk more later?"

"Of course my dear . . . when you are ready. You must be weary from your travels."

William hurried to open the parlor door, meeting Melanie and the crying child.

"Excuse me . . . Sir. Is Ethan's mother within?"

From a few feet behind her father, Teresa Anne answered, "I'm coming. Poor Ethan must be famished. Let's go upstairs."

When William arrived in Vicksburg, it had the uncommon appearance of a ghost town. Few people were out and about, and the usually busy dock was practically empty. Going directly to the seed purveyor's establishment, it seemed odd no one was outside waiting to enter. Usually full of buyers dickering over prices and looking for bargains, he was confused by the quiet atmosphere, beginning to wonder if the place was even open. With guarded trepidation he opened the door and approached the unattended counter. Raising his voice, he hollered, "Where the hell is the proprietor?"

From a backroom someone yelled back, "Who it be?"

William replied curtly, "Show yourself first; then I'll be saying."

Peeking through a crack in the partially ajar door, the proprietor cautiously quizzed, "Is it you, William?"

Answering with a slight degree of annoyance, "What's going on? I've never seen the town like this."

"Haven't you heard? We's got Yellow Jack . . . really bad it is too."

"Yes, I've heard. I'll be out of here tomorrow."

"William, I'll not sugar coat it. It's real bad, and people are scared. It's spreading like wildfire. The worst part . . . no one's knowin' how or when it's goin' to get 'em. It's a true conundrum . . . I'm thinkin'."

"Well then, I need to buy seed and make arrangements for its delivery. Once done, I'll be on my way."

"My seed's in short supply, and I'll be gettin' no more. They're afraid to come here, so you can have the last of it. I've sent my family packin'. Told them not to come back till this damn mess is done with. William, I'll give you a good price, cuz frankly, I reckon I can't rid myself of it. Something else, you won't find a crew to take the seed down river. You'll do best to get it loaded and go back with it."

"Is that why it's so damn quiet here abouts . . . no one's comin' and everyone's leaving?"

"More like dying. Can't bury 'em fast enough. Ran out of grave diggers too."

Momentarily lost in thought, William frowned before asking, "What does the sickness look like when it comes upon someone? I need to know what to look for . . . encountering a person who's got it."

"Best I hear, they start hurtin' all over. Especially, they gets a bad hurt in the head. It doesn't show itself at first . . . the yellow look. Best to stay away from anyone . . . even me."

They agreed on a price, and William paid him. Although the first time in years to pay in advance, the anticipated joy swiftly passed because of the dire circumstances surrounding him.

"I'll have the sacks laid outside for you by early morn."

When William held out his hand to shake on the completed transaction, his offer was declined. "I best not. Hope you understand. Don't reckon you should shake with anyone around these here parts. William, get yourself goin' as fast as you can." Dipping his head, the proprietor added, "Here's wishin' we meet again in a year's time. Good luck to ya."

Later in the afternoon, William asked the barkeep to help secure men to carry the seed to the dock early the following day. Saying, "I'll be indebted to you kind sir if perhaps you might roundup twice as many as I'll be needing." Finishing his last whiskey in the almost empty saloon, William placed a silver dollar on the bar—more than enough for his several whiskeys—and a bonus for the barkeep's trouble.

As promised, the bags were stacked and waiting early the next day. And as William anticipated, about half of the men showed . . . most either hung over or still intoxicated. There was no conversation among them as they hurried to move the bags to the dock . . . except for those who slowly staggered along behind the others. He had promised to pay them half to show up and move the seed to the dock; the balance when the seed was loaded onto the boat.

However, he'd purposely failed to mention that the boat would not be waiting at the dock until later in the day.

When dropped off at Vicksburg, he clearly remembered the boat captain's words. "I'll return at high noon . . . neither sooner nor later in one day's time." While stepping off the boat, the captain added, "I'll be stopping just long enough for you to jump on . . . no longer."

Explaining the situation to the workers, they weren't keen on hanging around till noontime. While they mulled it over—whether to stay or leave—he reminded them of their final payment due when the seed was onboard the boat. Some demanded payment in advance for returning, but in the end they walked away grumbling but did agree to come back.

Watching the loaders leave, William prayed they would return, prayed the boat would come back for him, and prayed his precious seed would be allowed on the boat.

Fearful the boat would be early, William left to get a quick bite to eat. After finishing a hasty meal of hog jaw and grits in the empty boarding house dining room, he rushed through the purchase of some of the items on his wish list. Still afraid of missing the boat and receiving no assistance, he was forced to lug his newly acquired possessions and his personal bag himself. Huffing and puffing, he finally placed everything together on the dock and scanned the water upriver. Feeling better and assured all was in order and ready, he sat down and leaned against the seed sacks and waited . . . constantly swatting at the flittering flies and mosquitoes—many stinging him before being smashed or shooed away.

At half past noon, the men arrived about the same time he saw the boat approaching . . . giving William cause to wonder if they were somehow watching from afar.

Pleading with the boat operator to take the seed, William offered him twice the usual amount for his trouble. The operator finally agreed but was openly irritated. Once the seed was stacked on the boat and the loaders paid, William walked over to the captain, saying, "I'm beholdin' to you sir for your assistance to my plight. I won't forget your kindness."

"My good deed will do me no good if I get touched by the Yellow Jack. The stories I've heard are right down gruesome. The worst part is not knowin' how you gets it. These here parts are mostly deserted. I won't be back to this neck of the woods soon. Goin' to stay in New Orleans till it's considered safe to venture north. If I didn't know you from years past, you'd be stuck here. That being a true fact."

# Chapter 15

$\mathcal{A}$bigail was somewhat aware of William leaving Willowland. He visited her . . . saying something about seed and Vicksburg. But since she no longer sought his assistance, she really didn't care where he went or what he did. In fact she didn't care about anybody or anything except escape. Fatigued beyond description and with no energy to fight off the demons trying to harm her, she welcomed her flight into dreams of happier times. Since no one could help her and realizing early on the impossibility of helping herself, she willing took the potion . . . even demanding it. Only the opium could separate her from the evil ones. So, rather than hide from the dead bodies, the snakes, and the spiders . . . but mostly from Kizzi, she willingly took the potion and drifted away.

Out of the shadows, Teresa Anne's face came into being . . . intermingled within her sleep and awake times. During the murky in-between periods, she saw her daughter as a little girl full of laughter; then sometimes, a grown up Teresa Anne's face staring back at her with tears of sadness. Matilda often visited, as well as her father and mother, but when she looked for them—seeking advice or assistance— they couldn't be found. When awake, the chills had gotten worse and the oozing bumps on her arms itched. No amount of blankets or scratching gave her relief.

Teresa Anne was in and out of her mama's room throughout the day and into the late evening. Worried and exasperated by her mother's condition, she was determined to spend as much time as possible by her bedside. She thought by doing so, she could find answers for her mother's weird behavior. Even though Daddy had explained in horrific detail about her mama's mood changes and bizarre actions, she refused to concede Mama had gone stark-raving mad . . . as he suggested. She was determined to search for another explanation. However, each time she left her mama's room, she felt more perplexed than ever.

Perhaps the potion was making Mama behave this way, she considered. But when she gave her less, she became irritated, wanting to get out of bed and run across the room.

Once while reading the Bible to her, Abigail slipped out of bed and tried to climb out the window. Noticing her body looked frail and malnourished—just skin and bones—Teresa Anne marveled at her mother's strength. Unable to know what to do, how to make her eat, or how to keep her safe, she gave her more potion and cried in helplessness. From then on she asked the attendant to remain in the room while she was there with her mama. Having previously told each attendant to leave, so she could be alone with her; she changed her mind when it took both of them to get her back into bed.

In desperation Teresa Anne tried to engage her mother in conversation, even venturing back to happy memories of past times. Nothing she tried or said brought her back in touch with reality. On one occasion she came fairly close to having a normal reaction . . . mentioning Ronald's excitement about receiving his first pony at Christmastime. "Remember Mama, her name was Precious. Mama, do you remember Precious?"

The reply was odd but at least she received a partially sensible answer. "I saw her last night, running wild under the window . . . fast too . . . a flowing white streak bounding into the willows." Beyond Teresa Anne's understanding . . . how could her mother believe she saw Precious? Well, at least Mama remembered the pony was pure white with a long flowing white tail.

Before leaving her mama's room to retire for the night, Teresa Anne asked the attendant to closely watch over her. Feeling some-what foolish for the request, of course they would look after her. Father told her not to worry about her care while he was away; explaining all of the attendants had been carefully watching to her mother's needs for months. When Teresa Anne bent down and kissed her mother's forehead, she clearly heard her say with-out opening her eyes, "It's my fault. I'm damned. I wish for hell and punishment." Teresa Anne left without saying another word. Although speechless, her body continued to shake until entering her bedroom across the hall.

As Teresa Anne prepared for bed, she didn't know how her father watched his wife's decline day in and day out . . . observing her sanity slipping away before his very eyes. But then, what could he do? What could she do? What could anyone do? How was it possible for Mama to change from a loving, caring, and normal person to becoming . . . ? Although she tried, it was impossible to put a name to what her mother had become.

Rocking Ethan to sleep, she didn't feel he was adjusting very well to being away from home. He'd been fussing and whining all day. Nothing seemed to make him happy. Thank goodness for Melanie's attention to his every whim. Only one day at Willowland and she was exhausted. Once Ethan was sleeping soundly, she looked forward to a much needed good night's rest.

Looking down at Ethan's peaceful face, she carefully carried him to his bed. Watching for a minute to make sure he seemed comfortable, she hastened to her bed, snuggling into the goose down pillow and was quickly asleep.

Awakened in the early hours by Ethan's cries, Teresa Anne sat up in bed, not certain at first where she was. As she threw her legs over the side of the bed, she glimpsed a wispy figure in a white gown standing over Ethan's bed.

"Melanie, why is Ethan crying?" she asked. Looking down and sliding into her slippers, she asked again. Standing, and even though Ethan was no longer crying, she still expected an answer. As she stepped forward, the figure seemed to float toward the closed bedroom door . . . then strangely disappeared. Blinking her eyes and running her hand through a patch of matted hair, she thought . . . good Lord, I must have been dreaming . . . even walking in my sleep. Was Ethan really crying or were his cries also part of her dream? Still questioning herself and just in case Melanie was in the room earlier and imagined during the dream, she opened the door and looked down the hall in both directions. Sure enough, Melanie was in the hall but not walking away . . . but rather walking toward her. Noticing her night garment was blue instead of white, it was most definitely a stupid dream. But even with the certainty of the dream being stupid, it was nevertheless peculiar, she thought.

"Madam, is Ethan all right?" Melanie asked. "I heard him crying and was on my way to see about him. You seemed very tired when you retired earlier. I wanted to come and settle him for you."

"Were you in my room a minute or so ago . . . even earlier?" Teresa Anne inquired.

"No, Madam."

"I must have been dreaming. Yes, indeed I was. You are correct; I am very tired."

"Would you like me to take Ethan, so you can rest?"

"Thank you but he has quieted down. So, you heard him crying too?"

"Yes, Madam."

"Goodnight Melanie."

"Goodnight Madam."

Returning to her room, Teresa Anne could not stifle the feeling that something wasn't quite right. Looking down at Ethan, he was quiet but squirming with an occasional off and on faint whimper. Not wanting to return to the habit of nursing him during the night, she picked him up, hoping to quickly rock him back to sleep. Almost falling asleep herself, she was finally able to lay him down but this time in bed next to her.

Once back in bed herself, it took some time for her to completely relax, continuing to go back over what had happened earlier. Was it worrying too much about her mother? Maybe the lack of sleep had her on edge . . . affecting her senses. How she wished her husband was by her side to give comfort, support, and understanding.

Waking to Ethan's normal morning cry, Teresa Anne rubbed her eyes, dismissing the previous night's episode. Refreshed, she picked Ethan up, showering him with kisses and baby-talk. Laying him back down for cleaning before nursing time, she noticed a whelp across his face. Thinking he'd scratched himself last night in his sleep—perhaps causing him to wake crying—she needed to bite his nails down.

Finishing her morning personal care routine and nursing Ethan, she handed him to Melanie before saying, "He seems to be having a better day today."

Going directly to her mother's room, she wished with all her heart to find her improved.

"Mama, good morning. Have you had your morning meal?" she asked, trying her best to sound cheerful.

Not expecting a response but still disappointed by the blank stare, she glanced over at a different attendant from the one present the previous night. "How is she today? Has she eaten anything this morning?" Teresa Anne asked, forcing herself to smile.

"She is the same . . . reckon she ain't goin' to get no better. As she do most times, she won't eat . . . maybe a little."

"Have you been taking care of her long?"

"No, Madam, just since harvest time past."

Hearing a knock at the door, Teresa Anne motioned for the servant to answer. Recognizing Melanie's voice, she said, "Melanie, come in."

"Madam, I'd rather not. Would you be so kind as to come out into the hall?"

Perturbed by Melanie's unusual manner—bordering on disrespectful—she replied, "Yes, but I'm not pleased with your request."

Seeing the frown on Madam's face, Melanie quickly said, "I beg your pardon. Could we go somewhere to talk alone? I must tell you something important to yours and Ethan's safety. I know of Ethan's bothersome night, but he's sleeping at the moment . . . his morning nap."

Without further conversation, Melanie followed Teresa Anne down the hall and into her mother's sitting room. Leaving Melanie in the middle of the room, Teresa Anne quietly closed the door to her mama's adjoining bedroom and sat down.

Feeling insecure, Melanie asked, "Might I sit?"

After receiving an affirmative nod, Melanie sat opposite her employer on a high-back chair and began, "Please do not fault me for what I am about to say. I would not . . . if I did not . . . oh Madam, you and Ethan could be in terrible danger. I have talked to some of the women watching after your mother, and they are convinced she is cursed."

"That is utterly impossible," Teresa Anne abruptly answered. Without pausing and slightly raising her voice, she asked, "Who told you such gibberish? My mother is a Christian woman who has spent her entire life reading and studying the Bible."

"Please Madam, hear me out. I ask again for you not to fault me for what I must tell you. I, myself, had perplexing feelings of doom—even evilness—come over me when we entered the plantation grounds."

"That is absurd. I cannot believe you are saying such utterances to me. This was my home, my parent's home, and my grandparent's home. It's always been in our family. To say there is evil here is . . . unacceptable. It is not your place to say such matters to me. Watch what you say. I don't care how pleased I've been with your service."

"Madam, I would not if I was not afraid for you and Ethan. When you saw me in the hall last night, something very menacing happened to me."

"Are you saying . . . when you saw me, something awful happened because of me?"

"Oh no . . . Madam, let me explain. On my way to see about Ethan's crying, a wave of chilling air came from the direction of your bedroom. Within seconds it lingered and seemed to wrap around my body before passing on. Your mother's servants have felt similar cold spells."

"Melanie, all of this talk is utter silliness. I don't want to hear any more of it."

"Momentarily lowering her head—an occurrence unlike her normal demeanor—Melanie said softly, "Please, I implore you. I have heard of this happening before. Perhaps I should start from the beginning . . . my beginnings. I have never told anyone of this . . . afraid of being rebuffed. Might I continue?"

"I will listen for a little while longer; then I must return to Mama's side."

"When I was a young child, I was—like my older sister—taken from our village by marauders. They were called invaders back then. They were cruel tribesman from a faraway village who sold people—their own kind—to slave marketers. While we huddled against our mother, my sister was yanked away first. I was hanging onto my mother's skirt—trying to hide—when they grabbed me. As I looked back for help, I saw my mother killed. The bad man used a long knife to slide it across her throat. When they pushed and dragged me through the thick brush, I passed by my father's body. In the distance I heard my sister's screams for help. Sadly, I never saw her again. We were kept separated and sold by different bad men."

"How awful for you and your family."

"I want to tell you everything; then you'll know all the truth. There is more. Maybe when I finish, you will understand. My mother was a Voodoo Priestess, but it was called Voudon then."

Melanie's statement was barely out of her mouth, when Teresa Anne gasped and asked, "What does any of this have to do with Willowland Manor or my family? We have never or would never have anything to do with devil worship."

Lowering her head and speaking quietly in an apologetic manner, "I don't know, but your mother shows the same signs as others I've heard of . . . ah . . . cursed."

Like a flash, her mother's words replayed in her mind. Words so despicable that she never wanted to recall them again. How could someone wish for hell and punishment? Not wanting to believe any of this, but her mother wasn't the same, acting tormented and hiding from things no one else could see. She had witnessed this herself. What if the ones watching over her mama were doing this to her, she briefly pondered.

"It is hard to believe any of what you're saying is happening, but if true, couldn't we all be in danger? Is it possible the women caring for my mama are to blame for her condition? Is that the reason why you didn't want to enter her bedroom?"

"Madam, I was told her condition started long ago, even before her trusted slave died. I believe her name was Matilda."

"Yes, my mother was extremely close to Matilda. I hope my father will be home soon. Surely he can help with this. Why are you telling me this . . . about your mother and all?"

"There is more to my beginnings. Should I continue?"

"Yes, of course. I'm listening."

I remember little of my life back then, but there was a lot of chanting and dancing. I remember my mother was considered very powerful—even worshiped as a queen—but some were frightened of her too. Once I arrived in America, I was fortunate to be secreted away with other girls my age. A Baptist preacher saved us. We were placed in homes in the north where we did chores to earn our keep. We weren't paid but were fed, clothed, and sent to school. We were also made to attend church. Eventually, I came to believe in Jesus Christ as my redeemer."

"Melanie, you haven't answered my question. Why didn't you want to go into my mother's room?"

Ignoring the direct question again, Melanie continued. "Many of the girls didn't want to learn English and still believed in the old ways, searching out those who practice in the spirit world. They sought the invisible spirits they thought could do good—like healing—but could also do harm—like cursing others. There are those who still practice Black Magic, believing they can place death curses on others who have done them wrong in one way or another. After being told that both good and bad spirits can be passed down through generations, especially from a Priestess to her children and those following, I was frightened for most of my younger life. I prayed constantly for strength if this should ever come to me. Once baptized, I put those worries behind me and became content."

Shaking her head, Teresa Anne remarked, "I do not understand any of this."

"When there is no other reason for cold air to appear, spirits can cause the chill. It can be a sign they are present. Not that a person is cursed when this happens, but it can show itself when this happens. I prayed all night. I could not forgive myself if I didn't talk to you. Madam what if the spirit passed through me while coming from your room?"

"Melanie, you must tell me why you didn't want to enter my mama's room, and why you are afraid for me and Ethan?"

"I was told your mother is covered with boils, sees invisibles, and talks in riddles. I've been told this is what happens to one who's cursed. That is why I'm frightened and don't want to enter your mama's room. Though forbidden to practice openly, Voodoo still exists for those who believe. Because of my mother, I once believed. I don't want to consider it's possible, but I'm scared. After I felt the chilling and saw the mark on Ethan . . . ."

"What mark on Ethan?"

"Did you not see the scratch on his face?"

Dismissing any evil connection to her innocent child, Teresa Anne replied, "Yes, he needs his nails chewed down." After a long and thoughtful silence, she asked, "Why my mama? Why her?"

"I have tried to learn of a reason. I've been told she must have done something of life or death consequences to cause such suffering cast upon her . . . maybe even more than one life. Madam, could we leave when your father returns. I beg of you."

"I must think on it. Maybe if true—and I'm not saying it is— we can do something to help her. Are you sure she is safe with the women watching her?"

"They have sworn to me—under God's name—that they mean her no harm."

"Perhaps they are saying so in order to keep their positions within the manor."

"Madam, if it eases your mind, the new supervisor is a man of Christ. He has started regular church services every Sunday. To their understanding—the ones watching after your mama—no Voodoo is practiced on or near the plantation. The workers talk among each other, and many are afraid for their own selves."

"I will talk with Father as soon as he returns. I will also keep Ethan in bed with me at night. You must never leave him alone during the day. Do you understand?"

"Yes, Madam. I forgot to tell you. The potion seems to make it harder for the spirits to control her. I am sorry to put this weight upon you."

As they stood to leave, Teresa Anne's thoughts revisited her peculiar dream and then fixated on her mama's awful words.

# Chapter 16

William stepped onto the dock at Willowland, happy to be back safely for many reasons. After the last two grueling and stressful days, the boat ride had been problem free and uneventful. Sleeping through most of the trip and waking just a few miles from home, he felt surprisingly rested. Most importantly, he had accomplished bringing home the seed, so planting could commence on schedule. Although unable to purchase his entire wish list, he'd luckily procured the last two available bottles of his favorite whiskey.

After thanking the captain again for his consideration, he told him, "My workers will be down to unload the seed within the hour." Since the original plan was for his return to be the following day at the earliest, he didn't expect his people to be waiting but apologized to the captain anyway for the poor planning. In order to minimize the waiting time and wanting to move on as quickly as possible, the boat crew willingly pitched the seed bags onto the dock. Normally, he would have been irate watching a bag split open when it landed, but under the circumstances, he remained quiet.

Although his time away had not turned out as hoped, he realized it could have been a lot worse. Feeling fine, he was extremely grateful and confident he'd skirted the dreaded Yellow Fever, and a reason in itself to be thankful.

Watching the boat leave, William held tightly onto the bag holding his new whiskey and carefully stepped over the broken bag, trying to ignore the spilling seed. While walking toward the manor and almost halfway there, Jefferson ran to his side.

"Welcome back Boss."

"Thank you. I'm pleased to be back," William answered with a smile.

"Should I saddle your horse and brung it to you?"

"No, the walk feels pleasant. Would you tell the supervisor of the waiting seed? Mention to be cautious since one bag is already broken; the seed scattering. And Jefferson, my garment bag should to be gathered to the house."

"Yes, Boss."

William picked up the pace, looking forward to a home cooked meal, talking with Teresa Anne, and glimpsing a peek of Melanie once again from afar.

Entering the eerily quiet manor, William hollered, "I'm home. Where is everyone?"

Bessie appeared from the dining room, saying as she rushed to him, "Wees not expectin' youse till tomorrow. Where be youse holdin's?"

"They are on the dock and will be here in due time."

"Can I's take what youse carryin'?"

"No, Bessie. I will take this to the library myself." Giving her an obvious wink, he added, "Two bottles of my favorite whiskey."

"Can I doos anything more for youse, Massa?"

"You can tell me where my daughter is?"

"She be yonder with Mistress upstairs."

"Thank you. That will be all."

As William walked into the library, he marveled at how little he'd thought about Abigail while gone. Although his main concern was directed at acquiring seed, he'd purposely wanted to distance himself from his wife. In reality he had already done so long ago. If not for the cloud of Yellow Fever hanging over Vicksburg, he would have liked to stay longer. Looking forward to escaping Abigail's illness and the accompanying insecurity of never knowing what she'd do or say, his time away was too short. Now home and unaffected by the fever, he would need to face her once again and probably more often because of his daughter's presence. Perhaps Teresa Anne would enlighten him on her observations of her mother's behavior. Since she'd be looking at the problem from a fresh perspective, maybe she'd see the situation with clearer eyes.

Taking a deep breath, William unlocked the whiskey cabinet, removed the last bottle of whiskey, and with a final gulp straight from the bottle, swallowed the last of it. Carefully placing the new bottles into the cabinet, he smacked his lips together and headed upstairs.

Knocking on Abigail's closed bedroom door, he heard Teresa Anne's voice say, "Yes?" As he answered, "It's your father," he opened the door with hesitation on what he was about to see. As he entered, he didn't look in the direction of Abigail's bed, preferring to look everywhere else. He glanced at the servant, the floor, the wallpaper, and finally at Teresa Anne.

"Daddy, you're home early."

"Yes, Darlin'. How are you doing?" he asked pleasantly.

"I'm not exactly sure how to answer your question. It's difficult to say. Mama is the same, and it's horrible."

His answer would have nothing to do with his wife because he wasn't ready to approach that particular subject yet. "I'm very hungry. Could we dine like old times—except for your mama not being present—and visit about your family and better times?"

"That would be nice. Give me about an hour. Does Sallie know we'll be sitting for supper?"

"She will as soon as I tell her. I'll stop by the kitchen before seeking out my supervisor. I look forward to a proper meal with you."

"Daddy, don't you want to say hello to Mama?" Teresa Anne asked quietly.

Knowing he should or Teresa Anne wouldn't understand, William walked to Abigail's bedside. He had not seen his wife in probably a week's time, other than briefly telling her of his leaving. Even then, he'd not directly looked at her. Looking down, he was immediately repulsed by what he saw. Her lips were puffed with large bumps scattered across them—some covered with bloody scabs—and her skin had darkened at least two shades with thick deep wrinkles under the eyes. Wanting to look away, he knew

117

Teresa Anne wouldn't be satisfied unless he addressed Abigail before leaving.

"Abigail, can you hear me?" he asked. Without response, he tried again. "Abigail, open your eyes. It's William."

As he turned to leave, she answered, "I can't see you through the gray smoke."

Looking across the room in Teresa Anne's direction, William replied, "Abigail, there is no gray smoke present in this room."

Her answer was short, "Liar."

Walking past Teresa Anne, he mumbled, "See you at supper." Without looking back, William hurried out of the room.

Trying his best to shrug off the lingering sight of Abigail's face and distance himself from anything pertaining to her, he headed for the kitchen.

Entering the kitchen, he hoped to encounter Teresa Anne's servant. Uncertain why he was drawn to her—who was he kidding . . . surely not himself—she was like a replica of Kizzi's mother. Not mentioning her name since her death—the name he gave her—he said it over and over in his mind . . . Venus, Venus, Venus.

"Sallie, whatever you're fixing, it sure smells wonderful. I'm sure looking forward to your vittles . . . whatever they be. When it comes to a scrumptious spread for a hungry man, you sure do a right fine job."

"I knews you'd be missin' my cookin'. I dressed a fresh hen soon as I hears you come home."

Stepping out the backdoor, he'd already put any thoughts of Abigail away, replaced with others of Venus long ago. Looking for Benjamin's whereabouts, he wanted to make sure the seed had been placed safely in storage, reminding himself to inquire about Benjamin's plans to go north for his family.

It was time for supper, and William could hardly wait. Trying to be patient while waiting for Teresa Anne to join him, he looked around the dining room. Gazing at the dining table, he was both pleased and impressed. It had been a long time since their best china was laid out, complete with the good silverware and crystal glassware. He could not remember the last time a centerpiece of fragrant flowers adorned the table.

As William pulled out the chair for Teresa Anne, he remarked, "You look mighty fetching daughter and the table looks lovely. Thank you."

"I wanted to do something special for old times' sake and since Mama . . . ."

"Time has changed many things here at Willowland but not my love for you."

"Unfolding the linen napkin and placing it on her lap, Teresa Anne smiled before replying, "I love you too."

"On a happy note, the plantation is once again profitable," he offered.

Waiting until after Bessie removed their empty sweet potato soup bowls, Teresa Anne asked, "Daddy, when did you notice Mama wasn't quite the same?"

"Must we discuss it now? Might we just have a pleasant supper? I've had a harried two days and would like to enjoy a pleasing meal with my daughter."

While Bessie placed the main course before them, Teresa Anne withheld comment. Patiently waiting until Bessie was out of the room, she noticed her father's concentration on each item as it was placed on the table.

"Daddy, you act as if this is a new experience for you."

"Sadly, it is. I grew tired of eating alone. I'm not ashamed to say I've been taking my meals in the kitchen . . . just eating and quickly moving on. You can't imagine how much I've truly missed this."

"Poor dear Daddy, I wish I could stay longer, but I need to return home soon. That is why I'd like to discuss Mama before I leave."

After moving the meat platter closer and sinking a serving fork into a chicken leg, William asked, "Could we eat first?"

Without replying, Teresa Anne lowered her head, wondering how to approach what she'd talked about with Melanie. It wasn't going to be easy but neither would it be fair to leave without discussing their conversation. She could not bring herself to talk about her own peculiar dream . . . now beginning to wonder if it was a dream or frightfully real. Each time she thought of it, she quickly dismissed it as imagined . . . too afraid to give it the least bit of credibility.

During the meal, William asked about Ethan, asked about her husband's business, asked about the staff's cooperation during his absence, and finally asked general questions about her servant,

Melanie. They discussed his trip, and he mentioned the problems associated with the sickness surrounding the town . . . even mentioning his relief at not being affected by it.

After finishing two pieces of pecan pie and patting his stomach, William said to Bessie while she cleared the table, "That was one fine meal. Please relay my compliments to Sallie. Tell her I said she prepared an excellent meal."

As William pulled away from the table, Teresa Anne said sternly, "Daddy, don't you go leaving now. We need to address Mama."

"I was thinking on taking a short nap. Can't it wait until later?" he asked sheepishly.

"I've already been waiting. What better time than now while we're alone without ears listening."

"All right. If we must, then let's get on with it. I'm thinking there's nothing to say on the subject."

Teresa Anne started slowly, discussing the actions of her mama . . . ones William was already quite aware of. After at least thirty minutes of give and take on suggestions and different possibilities on how to proceed, Teresa Anne said, "Daddy, I need to discuss a possibility that will be hard for you to believe. I'm not even sure I believe it, but it does make some sense, especially since nothing else does. Before I begin, I'll use the same words Melanie used with me before she began. Please don't fault me for what I'm about to tell you."

Closely watching her father's expressions while she spoke, he had the same reaction she'd had . . . utter disbelief, confusion, and shock. But it was the look on his face after she answered his question, "Why does Melanie know such things?" which took the color out of his face.

"Daddy, after all I've told you, why are you not surprised— perhaps even upset— about Melanie's mother being a Voodoo Priestess?"

"Because I think I bought her sister many years ago. She died."

"I'm sure there were many Voodoo Priestesses, their children, and followers sold as slaves to plantations all over the South."

"No, as soon as I saw her, she was a dead ringer to her sister."

"Daddy, think on it. Was it before or after she died when Mama started changing?"

"No, no. She died not long after I purchased her. When I brought her to Willowland, it was before the war. Everything was good then with Abigail and with our family."

"How did she die? Was there an accident? Did she work in the house?"

"She died during childbirth. She had a daughter, and I kept her on the plantation. She was used to help Matilda inside the house."

"Which one is she? Does she look after Mama?"

"She ran away. I don't know why. Her leaving never made any sense to me."

"Melanie hasn't been able to learn anything from the women who care for Mama. I'm at a loss to know what to do. Has anything strange happened to you since Mama changed?"

"No, not to me, but my overseer left without notice . . . just up and disappeared."

"I was told possibly Mama did something of life and death consequences to make this awful result fall upon her. Daddy, wouldn't you know of such a terrible happening?" With no response from her father and full of apprehension, Teresa Anne asked, "Can you think of anything to cause her to be cursed . . . if that's even possible?"

"Can't say I do. Your mama pretty much ran the house with a strong hand. I mean, she'd get angry and dismiss household people. Maybe yelled at a few now and then, even sent a few packing, but nothing so bad to cause a curse on her. What am I saying? This is all too preposterous to give any sensible credence to it. All of this Voodoo talk is just talk . . . searching for an answer when there is none. Your mama hasn't been the same since the war, since losing the boys, since times were hard with no social events in her life, and since Ronald's death. She just gave up when Ronald passed. It's all been too much for her to handle. That's what I'm thinking. The other is too outrageous to consider . . . much less believe."

"Daddy, you are absolutely right about her unhappiness and depression. I saw how devastated she was at Ronald's funeral. However, this seems different to me. I would stay longer if I thought I could help, but I give up. I can neither understand nor make it any better. Best I go home and be a good wife and mother. Ethan is not comfortable here."

"I understand you have another life and family to tend to; I surely do. I cannot thank you enough for coming."

"I love you, Daddy. I'll be here another day or so to set up arrangements for my travels home. Once I'm gone, you must promise to post any changes occurring with Mama."

# Chapter 17

*I*t had been a week since William's return home and three days since Teresa Anne's departure. At William's urging Benjamin left immediately to relocate his family to Willowland. Although Benjamin assured him all would be fine during his absence, William still felt the importance of being out and about the plantation, especially where the field workers gathered to work.

Beginning the morning following Benjamin's parting—rising unusually early to ring the morning work bell—William could barely move his arms or legs to dress. Plagued by a multitude of aches and pains, he passed his body's discomfort off to the numerous times he'd been on and off his horse to touch the readiness of the plowed ground for planting. Just the second day of Benjamin's absence, and he already missed him, feeling weary and useless to direct the workers. If he remembered correctly, Benjamin would not be returning for at least another three days at the earliest, giving him to wonder if his tired old body could survive until then.

While doing the least amount necessary to get through the day, by early afternoon his head was pounding and wouldn't let up. Walking slowly into the kitchen, he waited for Sallie to notice him. Clearing his throat to catch her attention, she finally looked up; her face showing surprise to see him. She smiled before asking, "Massa, youse wants supper early?"

"Not early . . . not at all. I'm not hungry."

"What's the matter with youse; youse always hungry," answered with a chuckle.

"Do you have a cure for a hurting head and hurting body?"

"Massa feelin' poorly?" she questioned with a frown.

"Yes, I think I'll retire early."

"While the sun's a shinin'? Maybe youse special whiskey make youse better."

Painfully moving his head from side to side, William answered quietly, "Good night."

Tilting her head, Sallie watched him leave . . . all the while quickly shaking her head back and forth in disbelief.

Going directly to his bedroom, William struggled to remove his boots. Too fatigued to change into night garments, he fell onto the bed and was immediately asleep. Sometime in the early hours of the morning, the chills started, and he vomited. "Dear God, it must be the fever," he said out loud, while his thoughts considered . . . what to do . . . what to do? Did he infect Teresa Anne, or Ethan, or both? What about the others he'd come into contact with? Strangely, he didn't consider Abigail as he thought about those he'd talked to after arriving home. Did he get it from someone in Vicksburg—of course he did—deciding it could have come from anyone there. Sorry he didn't get more information about the fever—but in a hurry to flee with the seed—his mind was set on getting back home as quickly as possible. Shivering, he lit a candle to see if his skin was yellow. No, it wasn't. Maybe he was suffering from a different malady? Going back to bed, he piled the covers over him and finally went back to sleep.

Sallie was the first to notice that Massa hadn't come down for breakfast. She'd already prepared a plate for Mistress and one for the helper staying in her bedroom. Massa's daughter make it clear while here and again before she left—two meals, three times a day—should be sent upstairs. It seemed important to Massa's daughter for the attendant not leave her mother's side even to eat.

Leaving the kitchen to look for Bessie, she found her pacing back and forth outside Massa's bedroom.

"What's youse doin'?" Sallie asked, confused by her odd behavior.

"I's don't knows. I's don't knows. What to doos? What to doos?" she answered.

"What youse sayin' girl?" Sallie questioned.

"I's goes in like I doos ever day . . . to start cleanin' and such. Massa hidin' under the beddin' and hollers at me, 'Get out quick. Shut the door.' He never done nothin' like this before. Maybe he gots what Mistress gots?"

"He eats no supper meal. I fixed fried rabbit too," Sallie remarked with annoyance.

"Um, um, um . . . this ain't no good," Bessie replied.

"Guessin' we best get along with our business and sees what happens. I gots lots to do in the kitchen," Sallie remarked with a shrug.

By noontime Sallie stopped outside Massa's room and listened with her ear against the door. Hearing nothing and deciding it

must be real bad for Massa—having never acted this way before—
she left to find the outside boss. With no answer at his cabin door,
she knocked at each cabin until someone finally answered. A pregnant worker told her, "He gone to gets his family. Maybe he'll be
back tomorrow . . . can't rightly say."

"Who be in charge with the worker boss gone?" Sallie asked.

"I hears the master of the house been seein' to the workers.
Whys you askin' me such questions? Who you be?"

Without answering, Sallie asked, "Doos the worker boss man
have a helper?"

"Yes, he do. His name is Jefferson. Is he in trouble?" Not
waiting for a response, she quickly let Sallie know she knew who
she was talking to when she harshly remarked, "If it's Jefferson you
be after, best stay in the house where you belong and tend to your
own doin's."

Without answering Sallie left to think on what to do next.
It didn't seem like a good idea to wander the fields in search of
Jefferson, choosing to return to the house and think more on the
problem. Looking back, Sallie glimpsed the woman standing outside her cabin and closely watching her every step.

Once inside, she sought out Bessie again, whispering, "Is he
out?"

"No, I's never seen nothin' like it. Let's knock on the door.
Youse do it."

Frowning but agreeing, Sallie walked to the door, all the
while making sure Bessie was following closely behind. Hesitantly
knocking while saying, "Massa, youse all right? Want me to brung
you sump'n to eat . . . maybes chicken soup?" After a long pause

and looking at each other, Sallie knocked again and said louder, "Massa, is youse all right?"

This time, she received a faint reply and thought she heard, "Go away. I'm sick." Perhaps she heard but wasn't certain, "Save yourself."

Too distant from the door to hear the reply, Bessie looked at Sallie questionably. Shaking her head at Bessie, Sallie said in an equally loud voice, "I's fix you some peppermint tea and chicken soup." Turning to Bessie, she said, "I's gonna fix it and gives youse a holler. Whilst youse take it?"

"I's not enter if he say nay but will knock and leaves it."

For the next few hours Sallie cooked, and Bessie listened at his door. Rushing through the soup preparation—starting with catching and killing the chicken—Sallie wondered what to do about supper. The Mistress needed to be fed—not like she ate much—and also the others in the house. She stopped a moment to pray Massa would be better and want supper too. She missed those days—now long gone—when Mistress planned the daily meals or sometimes a week in advance. She liked the fixin' but not the plannin'. Now she prepared whatever Massa said he had a hankerin' for.

While placing the soup and tea on a tray, there was a knock at the backdoor. Not wanting to be interrupted, she opened the door with a frown, finding Jefferson standing there with a quizzical look on his face. "What you want me for?" he asked.

"Wees got troubles. Massa sick and won't come out. Won't eat nothing since yesterday mornin'. Benjamin gone. What's to doos?"

"He not ring the bell this mornin'. I ain't seen him. Should I goes fors the doctor?" Jefferson asked but then answered his own question. "No, I hears he's dead from Yellow Jack."

"Where youse hear that?" Sallie questioned.

"From the boat worker taken Massa to Vicksburg. Says everybody's dead in Vicksburg."

"That not true. Massa no say so."

"Ain't you got somethin' to give him to make him better?" Jefferson asked.

"Don't reckon I's knows what's ailin' him," she replied apologetically.

"Just leave him be. He knows what's best. He'll come out when ready."

"When's youse boss man comin'?" Sallie asked, disappointed Jefferson couldn't help with the problem.

"Says he'll be back in a week's time."

"I's don't cares what he says, cuz I's don't knows when he leaves."

Jefferson looked down at his hands, touched his fingers, and counted before stating, "Three days."

"Maybes Massa be out and bout by then," she answered hopefully.

"I comes and sees back. Gots to go and do supervisin' for end of day till my boss gets back," Jefferson remarked proudly.

As Jefferson turned to leave, Sallie asked, "Who told youse bout me askin'?"

"That was me wife, Jasmine."

"Youse goin' to be a papa," Sallie offered with a smile.

With an air of pride and shyness, he answered back, "Reckon so."

"Go about your business then," Sallie said and closed the door.

Placing the reheated tea and soup back on the tray, she carried it out of the kitchen, finding Bessie sweeping the entrance hallway. Giving her a nod and without speaking, she carefully handed the tray to her. Waiting at the bottom of the stairs for news, Bessie soon appeared saying, "I done it. Now, we waits to see if he fetches it from the hall."

Benjamin, his wife, and two sons arrived at Willowland in the afternoon . . . three days later than originally planned. Jefferson met their wagon barely within the plantation grounds.

Slowing the wagon to almost a stop, Benjamin asked, "Jefferson, what's you doing? You should be out with the workers, not here waiting for me."

"Boss . . . stop. I need to tell you somethin'."

"No, my family is tired from traveling and needs to get settled." Clicking the reigns, Benjamin shouted, "Giddy up." Jefferson held up his hands and walked quickly in front of the wagon, forcing Benjamin to holler, "Halt" to the horses. Pulling the horses to a full stop, Benjamin yelled, "Jefferson, have you lost ya noggin during my absence?" Jefferson climbed onto the wagon rung, placing his mouth close to Benjamin's ear and whispered, "The Massa is dead."

"Did I hear you right?" asked with visible shock. "When?"

"This morning . . . best we knows."

"Stay where you be . . . hold on. We'll talk more when we get to the cabin."

As soon as they reached his cabin, Benjamin gave hurried directions for the family to start unloading and looked around; surprised to see a few field workers standing outside their cabins. Calling them forward to help with the unloading, he turned to Jefferson and asked, "Why are they not in the fields working?"

"I told them to stay behind . . . not knowin' if you'd be here today, needin' help with . . . youse know what."

"Where did it happen?"

"Inside the manor . . . in his bedroom."

Benjamin's first thought . . . the Mistress done him in. "What happened?"

"He gots real sick and quit eatin'. Rallied a day or so then turned yellow."

As if struck a hard blow to his stomach, Benjamin looked at those helping with the unpacking and at his family, saying hesitantly, "Yellow Jack."

"I reckon. The doc who helps us wouldn't step a foot into the house. We's told the real doctor in Vicksburg be dead."

"Anyone else sick?" Benjamin asked quietly.

"No, and Sallie says no one sick in the house except Mistress, and she only sick in the head."

Almost a month from the day she left Willowland, Teresa Anne received a post from Benjamin. Confused by the letter coming from Benjamin and not from her father, she instinctively knew the information inside wouldn't be good news.

> *Dear Madam,*
>
> *I regret to inform you of your father's passing. While I was collecting my family to Willowland Manor, your father became ill due from what I believe was the result of traveling to Vicksburg. I am not certain, but it doesn't appear any of the household people have the signs of the illness of Yellow Fever or Yellow Jack as most round here call it. By the time I returned, your father was already passed. Because of the nature of his sickness, no one would attend to him after his passing. I did the best I could under the considerations. He was buried in a plain box coffin and placed in your family's plot. I know this is not as it should be for a gentleman of his standing, but he was given a Christian burial, complete with a faithful preacher, hymns, and verses at the graveside. At present we are doing as we would if Mr. Wayland—may God bless his soul—was present but do need direction with your mother and the plantation. Please come as soon as you can.*
>
> *Yours in faith,*
> *Benjamin*

Teresa Anne looked for a date on the letter, wondering when this all happened. Daddy seemed fine when I left, she thought. After reading the letter and the original shock wore off; she read it again through tears rolling down her face. As she folded the letter, wanting to put it away until her husband came home, she saw a date on the backside. Why the letter took over two weeks to reach her was disappointing.

When her husband, Charles, came home early, he found her rocking Ethan and crying. Wondering if something happened to Melanie, he asked, "Are you all right? Why isn't Melanie attending to Ethan in the middle of the day?"

"She is out shopping. I must show you the letter I received today. Please help me decide what to do."

As he read the letter, his first comment, "I am terribly sorry about your father, but you are fortunate to have a trusted man like Benjamin present at the plantation."

"I don't want to go back there, but my obligation is to my mother. I know absolutely nothing about running the plantation. What should I do?"

"First things first. We need to know if we will be in jeopardy. Have you considered the likelihood of you, Ethan, or Melanie having already been infected?"

"Yes, and I'm terribly frightened of this possibility."

"I've heard the fever is raging in different parts along the Mississippi from New Orleans to as far north as Tennessee. Because of my banking interests, shipping has all but stopped . . . even some mail delivery. I will find out as much as I can, so we can come to a better decision. I have faith you won't put yourself or Ethan in danger. If safe to travel to Willowland, I will accompany you . . . helping in any way I can."

"Thank you Charles."

Teresa Anne had not discussed with Charles her lengthy bizarre conversation with Melanie or her own strange dream. Of late she'd decided it was definitely a dream and now felt silly to discuss it with anyone. She also considered Melanie's chilly feelings a figment of her imagination, brought on by her supposed childhood memories. She didn't doubt in the least that Melanie had unfortunately worked herself up to the point of believing her feelings were true facts.

# Chapter 18

When Teresa Anne and Charles arrived at Willowland, no one was waiting in front of the building nor inviting them inside at the door. As they entered the manor, Teresa Anne couldn't help but remember her previous visit and the excitement she'd felt coming home to see her mother and father.

Taking a moment to wait for a house servant to appear, Teresa Anne looked at Charles questionably before asking, "Where do you think everyone is?"

"Didn't you say your mother was never alone? Perhaps they're with her."

"Yes, but only in her room and not all of them. There are others: kitchen help, cleaning help, servers, and whatnot. Who will bring in our baggage?"

"We didn't bring much. I can attend to it," Charles replied but continued to look around.

"Don't be silly. I'll go to the kitchen. Surely I can find someone there," she replied before marching off.

When Teresa Anne entered the kitchen, she found three servants eating at the kitchen table. Sallie jumped up as if she'd encountered an intruder. Throwing up her hands in dismay before saying, "Oh Madam, I didn't knows youse comin'. Wees doin' nothin' wrong."

"It's all right. Your name is Sallie. Am I correct? I remember you from last time. You were very helpful to us . . . making special dishes for Ethan and all."

"Yes'm."

Bessie carefully rose from her chair and bowed before saying, "I'll goes to fixin' the room you settled in last. If it suits youse, Madam."

"That would be fine, but you should know my husband has accompanied me."

"Doos he wants another room from youse?" Bessie asked shyly.

"No, one room will do. If the small bed is still there, please remove it."

Looking back at Sallie, Teresa Anne asked, "Sallie, is there someone to gather our baggage? There is not much to bother with as we don't plan on staying long and did not bring Ethan."

The third person sitting at the table did not look up but rather lowered her head as if trying to hide. When Teresa Anne asked her name, she didn't answer right away and then spoke softly, "Daisy."

Speaking for Daisy, Sallie intervened and offered with an air of apology to justify Daisy's lack of engagement, "She watches after youse mama . . . been havin' a hard time of it."

Teresa Anne replied directly to Daisy, "Hello Daisy. I under-stand your watching after my mama is a difficult task."

Looking up with tears in her eyes, she answered in a frightened voice, "Hello, Madam."

"Daisy, aren't you supposed to be seeing to my mother and eating in her room?" Teresa Anne inquired.

"No, Madam. I was sent out by another."

"I don't understand. Then . . . why are you here in the kitchen? Do you have other duties in the house?"

"Before Daisy could answer, Charles stuck his head through the kitchen door and asked, "Did you forget about me?"

"I'm sorry, please forgive me. I guess I got carried away. Bessie is already upstairs preparing our room." Turning to Sallie, she reminded her of the baggage and also to let someone know the carriage horses would need tending to before saying, "We will be in my mother's room."

Without being addressed Daisy quietly said, "It is bad with your mama. I's sorry."

Teresa Anne nodded with compassion but wondered how it could be worse than when she left before. As they climbed the stairs, Charles stayed slightly behind. Not knowing where they were going other than upstairs, he followed Teresa Anne's lead down the hall. When they stopped outside her mother's room, Teresa Anne inhaled deeply and turned to Charles, "Remember what I told you on the journey here. It won't be a pretty sight so prepare yourself." Taking a second deep breath, she added, "I must also do the same." Not knowing exactly why, Teresa Anne knocked before opening the door. Perhaps it was to stave off the inevitable for a brief moment, she thought pensively. Even before taking her first step inward, the over-whelming stench smacked at her senses. Trying to take shallow breaths, she wiped her nose with a handkerchief and gave a small cough. Directly across from the door, a servant was sitting beside an open window but rose immediately as Teresa Anne and Charles walked into the room.

While awkwardly considering if she'd seen the attendant before, Teresa Anne gave her a nod before looking in the direction of her mother's bed. Taken aback by what she saw, her mama most certainly appeared worse than before . . . much worse. While Teresa Anne's eyes focused on the restraints tied around her arms and legs, she hesitantly moved closer. Within a few feet of her mother's bed, she heard hissing sounds and incoherent mumblings. When she looked back at Charles, he'd not moved an inch since entering, and his pale face spoke for itself. Still looking at Charles, all she could think of to say was, "She is much worse than when I saw her last." Turning to the attendant, Teresa Anne asked, "What has happened to my mama?"

"Wees ran out of medicine. She tries to kill Daisy this mornin' . . . tries to throw her out the window. Sniffling, she quickly added, "Wees need to keep the window open. She's sayin' bad things . . . awful things bout a person wees don't knows. Keeps sayin'. . . Kizzi. Madam, doos you knows Kizzi? Daisy says wees gots to tie her up to keep us . . . um, the Mistress safe."

What a lot to take in, Teresa Anne thought. How scary for Daisy. Although she'd never heard of anyone named Kizzi, she preferred not to discuss the attendant's remarks. Instead, she responded, "It's all right. I'm not angry with anyone; I understand. I truly do. I brought more medicine. Can you help me give it to her?"

"I'll tries, but she's very strong," she answered . . . clearly afraid.

Looking back at Charles, Teresa Anne asked, "Would you get the opium bottle from my big bag?"

"Where is it?" he asked, noticeably wanting to leave.

"The room directly across the hall from here. Please hurry."

As soon as Charles was out the door, Teresa Anne looked back at her mama . . . but closer this time. Her skin had darkened even more, her lips were now covered with continuous dry scabs, her exposed skin a mass of oozing boils, and her eyes were mere slits in an almost unrecognizable face.

Charles returned in due time with the opium but approached slowly to give the bottle to Teresa Anne. It was obvious he felt uncomfortable and didn't want to get any closer than necessary. Feeling her husband's uneasiness, she uttered, "Charles, we can do this. Would you see to our room . . . seeing to its orderly presence?"

As she watched Charles hurriedly leave, Teresa Anne couldn't help but wonder if he knew what she meant by her request. It didn't matter; she just wanted him out of her mother's room. In his haste to depart, Charles left the bedroom door wide open, so Daisy was easily noticed. She was standing quietly just out-side the door. Motioning for her to come inside and close the door behind her, Teresa Anne said, "Daisy, you did a good thing. Thank you."

"Can I help youse Mistress?" she offered.

"That would be good. Can you help us or tell me how to get the medicine safely into my mama without spilling it? It is hard to come by."

Even though Teresa Anne stayed until her mother quit jerking and hissing—seemingly settled down and sleeping—she didn't feel confident enough in her behavior to remove the restraints before leaving.

Stopping by her room, she expected to find Charles . . . maybe resting . . . but found a pregnant servant delivering a water pitcher and washing bowl. After saying, "Hello," she asked, "Did you perhaps notice where my husband went?"

"Yes, Madam. He tells me to bring these here and then goes downstairs to see Sallie in the kitchen."

"Thank you. What is your name?"

"Jasmine."

Entering the kitchen, Teresa Anne was surprised to find it empty. Before leaving to look elsewhere, Sallie came in through the backdoor. Somewhat out of breath, she asked, "Can I help youse with sump'n?

"No, Sallie. I was looking for my husband."

"I's shows him where to find the boss out yonder."

"Are you referring to Benjamin?"

"Yes, Madam." Pausing a moment, Sallie breathlessly continued, "I's been thinkin' and wonderin' bout youse little one . . . youse baby?"

"Thank you for asking. He's fine and staying at my home in Arkansas with Melanie. I know Arkansas sounds far away, but it really isn't."

"Sweet Lord Almighty. Thank the Lord. I's worried bout him cuz of the sickness and hims being so little."

"I was told no one around here became ill. Is that true?" Teresa Anne asked quietly.

"Yes'm. Wees prays and prays and the good Lord hears us. Wees all spared except Massa. May his soul rest in peace," Sallie answered, then closed her eyes for a moment.

"Yes, may his soul rest in peace. I truly miss him. My hope is he'll be proud of me . . . taking care of Mama and all."

"Youse Daddy sure loved youse. Talked bout youse alls the time before he passed . . . youse and Kizzi."

"Who is this Kizzi?" Teresa Anne asked. "I keep hearing her name."

Before Sallie could respond, Charles barged in through the backdoor, saying, "I had a good conversation with Benjamin. He is agreeable to your wishes."

Quickly yet thoughtfully, Sallie decided not to speak of Kizzie at the moment . . . maybe never. It would only lead to more questions, deciding it might never be the right time to discuss Massa's last words before he went into a deep sleep . . . passing soon after. No one else heard them because no one would go into his room to attend to him except her. She'd thought long and hard about what she'd heard, deciding it was not her place to judge him . . . it was up to the Lord. And it wasn't just the words he'd said but how he looked when he said them. She would never forget his laboring chest rising and falling, his tears glistening on yellow cheeks, or his final word uttered with a gasp . . . "Venus." She was naturally torn by what she'd heard and wondered why he'd told her such things. If her place to interrupt—which it wasn't—she was curious to ask if the Mistress knew. She would wait and see if Teresa Anne asked about Kizzi again. If not, she'd keep to her own business and speak nary a word of it to no one.

Speaking to Sallie, who looked far away in thought, Teresa Anne said, "Before I forget we will need breakfast early tomorrow. We will be meeting with Stone Bennington mid-morning."

"Yes, Madam."

Surprised she'd told a servant of her plans; it just seemed the right thing to do. She knew it had something to do with the multitude of problems the family and household help had suffered through together of late. She now had an understanding of why her mother felt close to Matilda, thinking she felt oddly and perhaps similarly close to Sallie—somewhat like family—yet she'd not known Sallie through the years like her mama knew Matilda. Of course she would never reveal these feelings to anyone . . . especially Charles. He'd think she'd gone crazy too.

Turning to Charles, she said, "I will check on my mother and then meet you in the parlor. We should finalize our plans for tomorrow's meeting."

Sallie asked, "Pardon Madam, when would you like supper?"

"Suit yourself. Have Bessie call us to the dining room. I know you were not expecting us . . . something easy to prepare."

"Thank you, Madam. Youse very kind."

Teresa Anne and Charles sat quietly while Bessie served them. Their meal consisted of a platter of fresh vegetables: sliced tomatoes, cucumbers, green onions, and radishes. Beside the vegetable platter was a bowl of pickled beets. Although odd to have stew for the main course, it was tasty—full of chicken, rice, and various

cooked vegetables. However, Teresa Anne concluded the best part
of the meal . . . the delicious biscuits. Considering them the best
she'd ever eaten, she ate two of the fluffy, buttery cakes. When
Sallie came into the dining room to apologize for not having time
to bake a pie, Teresa Anne took another one before Bessie cleared
the table and removed the biscuit plate.

Stone Bennington was nothing like Teresa Anne remembered.
He had a full white beard and a round body. After discussing pleas-
antries—like how she'd grown into a lovely young woman and the
many troubles the Wayland family had endured—he said, "I'm
interested in your plan . . . tell me more." He directed his question to Charles even though Teresa Anne felt it would be her wishes
which needed to be satisfied.

Although quite aware of it being a man's world, Teresa Anne
nevertheless considered herself the person responsible for her
mother and the land. After all, she was a Wayland.

Charles replied, "Teresa Anne's mother is ill and my wife does
not want to place her in an asylum. She wants her to live out her
life at Willowland Manor but doesn't want to live there herself or
be part of running the plantation. Neither do I. As per my post,
we are open to suggestions . . . especially since you are the largest
cotton grower in Mississippi."

Bennington cleared his throat and straightened in his chair. "I
will give you a fair proposition. Mind you, my offer is more than
right due to the respect I had for your wife's grandfather." Before

continuing, he looked directly at Teresa Anne. "We started with this land together many years ago—I was just a young lad then—but I always considered your grandfather my friend." Pausing as if remembering, he continued. "I will buy the land at fair market value. It will not include the manor or the accompanied out buildings. However, I would like to use the barn, worker cabins, and other necessary buildings in order to work the fields." Still looking directly at Teresa Anne, he said, "Your mama—your grandfather's daughter—can remain in her home until the end of her days. You can decide your wishes and how to proceed then. I'll not burden you with such matters now." He would never tell Teresa Anne about wanting to court her mama, but she only had eyes for William . . . wouldn't even give him the time of day. However, there was a time later on when they were very close, but that was long ago . . . and only for a few stolen and very secret moments. He would also not tell Teresa Anne that her grandfather had no use for William.

"Sir, you are most considerate," Teresa Anne answered. "Before we settle this transaction, I have a few requests for you to ponder. First, I would like your word to keep Benjamin on. He has been most helpful during these hard times, and my father said it was due to Benjamin's cotton expertise that the plantation has prospered."

With a nod Bennington replied, "I have heard nothing but good things about your supervisor. I have no problem with your wishes. In fact I welcome him and your workers. As the expansion will need them, they will be brought into my workforce."

"Thank you, Mr. Bennington."

"If I was making this deal with your grandfather, we would shake on it. However, and please take no offense, I will have my barrister draw up the contract. There is a matter of some hast involved because planting time is near. Looking first at Charles and then to Teresa Anne, he inquired, "Where should I contact you?"

Teresa Anne waited dutifully for Charles to answer. After glancing at Teresa Anne, Charles offered, "We will be returning to our home within a day or two."

"May I inquire where you reside?" Bennington asked.

"Well, you probably aren't familiar with the town's name, but it is called, Endora. It is located in Arkansas but close to the Mississippi border."

"I'm afraid I have not heard of it. Would you prefer the papers to be sent to you there?"

"No, Sir. My wife and I will return when the papers are ready for signing. We can discuss the final arrangements at that time. We have no doubt you will handle this in a just and gentlemanly fashion."

As the group stood in unison, Stone Bennington hastily rounded his desk to shake Charles's hand. As soon as Teresa Anne extended her arm, he genteelly bowed before placing a kiss on the back of her hand.

"Good day, Mr. Bennington," Teresa Anne said demurely.

"Good day, my dear," he answered with another bow.

Watching them leave, Stone remembered and then wondered—as he had for years—if perhaps Teresa Anne was his daughter. Neither here nor there but if true, she was not actually a Wayland but rather a Bennington. He continued to reminisce about stolen moments with Abigail long after her daughter's departure.

# Chapter 19

Returning from meeting with Stone Bennington, the mood at Willowland seemed different—not that the environment within the manor wasn't already subdued. Teresa Anne had the distinct feeling that somehow the staff knew what had transpired at the Bennington meeting. Perhaps her guilty conscious for selling the plantation contributed to her feelings. Even though the atmosphere was gloomy, she knew in her heart that she'd made the right decision to at least keep part of the plantation for her mama's sake. She honestly didn't know what the future would bring for the workers, especially the field workers, but at this point they would keep their jobs and positions. Down the line change would most certainly occur, but for now it was a finished arrangement . . . more or less. Her immediate task was to talk to Sallie and change her present responsibility from cook to house supervisor . . . if she was willing. It would be Sallie's decision if she still wanted to cook. The two of them needed to sit down and have a heart-to-heart conversation before she left for home. Hopefully, the outcome of their meeting would fulfill her immediate wishes.

The following day and after a quiet and somewhat somber breakfast, Teresa Anne asked Sallie to join her in the parlor as soon as possible. After a few minutes, Sallie arrived with an apparent air of unusual sadness on her face.

"Sallie, please sit." Noticing she was obviously distraught and uncomfortable, Teresa Anne said quickly and with a smile, "I want to thank you for all you do, helping to direct Mama's care and keeping the manor in order while more or less being on your own without supervision. I know it hasn't been an easy task."

Sallie answered, "Youse welcome," but her thoughts were wondering what the future would bring and what would happen to her and the others. Aware of Benjamin talking to Jefferson, she knew Jefferson told Jasmine. Then, Jasmine told everyone she met including Bessie. It was right before today's breakfast when she'd learned from Bessie about the plantation being sold to Stone Bennington. Feeling unappreciated, she was now certain she'd been the last person to know.

Sallie seemed far away in thought, so Teresa Anne cleared her throat before beginning. "Perhaps you've heard already that Mr. Bennington will purchase Willowland Manor but the cotton fields only." Quickly repeating, "The cotton fields only." Seeing Sallie look up with confusion, Teresa Anne added, "He will not own the house. The manor and the out buildings will remain Wayland possessions until Mama passes on. When she passes, a decision will be made on what to do with the remaining property. This will enable Mama to remain here until the end of her days. Sallie, do you understand?" Teresa asked calmly.

"I reckon. Might not for sures. Will youse be living here?" Sallie asked.

"No, my husband and I will return to our home; hence my reason for wanting to talk with you today. We felt it important for you to understand what was transpiring . . . ah, happening here at Willowland."

Remaining quiet for a moment to make certain Sallie understood, Teresa Anne waited for Sallie to ask more questions. When she didn't ask for additional information, Teresa Anne continued. "Very few things will change except I want to give you the position of household supervisor and raise your pay accordingly. Sallie, would you be willing to assume the responsibility?"

"I don't knows. I never been a boss or nothin' like such before," Sallie answered with an expression of concern.

"Well, you'll basically be doing what you're doing now, but it would give me peace of mind to know you would be in the position to give directions to see to Mama—making sure she is fed and taken care of until the end. I would count on you to supervise her day-to-day care. Watching after my mama would become your main concern. If you are not willing to take on this responsibility, I need to know now, so I can look further before I leave. Sallie, I feel confident you can manage this, because I've watched you already doing it. You can continue to cook or place another in the kitchen. It will be your choice."

"I's doos my best. I worries bout her medicine runnin' out. She not the same then."

"Do not be concerned or worry about the medicine. I'll visit periodically and bring more with me each time. One way or the other, I'll make sure you have medicine and money for incidentals . . . odds and ends you may need to buy. Myself or Charles will come monthly to pay you and the rest of the staff. That is our present plan, but of course I don't know how much longer my mama will endure. She has declined terribly since my last visit. Although Benjamin will work for Mr.

Bennington, he and the other workers will remain here on the plantation. The vegetable gardens, chicken and pig pens will still be available for you. We haven't worked out all of the details with Mr. Bennington, but I feel confident he will act in a just manner. He has given me his solemn promise, and it is my fervent prayer. I think it would be best if you close up most of the house. It would make Bessie's job easier. Let's see; I think I've covered the most important pieces. We'll be leaving tomorrow early, so if you have questions—and I'm sure you will— there will be time between now and then for you to ask."

"Madam, can I goes now?" Sallie asked hesitantly.

"Yes, but in a moment. I want to ask you one more question. Who is Kizzi?"

Halfway out of the chair, Sallie sat back down, took a large breath, and let it out slowly. "Madam, I's not want to cause youse no trouble, but the good Lord says to be truthful. I's not sure whys youse papa tells me such things, but maybes he's wantin' to get it out before he . . . before he meets his maker."

Giving Sallie time to wipe her eyes, Teresa Anne asked, "And this has to do with Kizzi?"

"Yes'm, it doos."

"And my daddy told you who Kizzi was?" Teresa asked with interest.

"Yes'm. Now mind youse, I's tellin' of youse daddy's words. Some ain't goin' to be pleasin' to hears or for me to be tellin'. Iffin' youse wants me to stop, holds up youse hand."

"I don't think there's anything you could say that would be news to me. Well, maybe about Kizzi. I've only just heard her name of late."

"Massa starts—youse daddy—sayin', 'I's have two daughters.'"
Sallie watched Madam grimace and waited to see if her hand went
up before continuing. "Then, he's talkin' bout youse and tea parties, Kizzi ridin' cotton sacks, and playin' games with Matilda. He
be smilin' real wide. I's thinkin' he's mixed-up in the head, cuz I
knows youse be his only daughter. Awful serious he be bout it, so
I stays quiet."

Sallie seemed to drift off in thought . . . perhaps trying to
remember his exact words. Full of dismay but a lot of curiosity
too, Teresa Anne asked, "Can you go on?"

"He starts talkin' of Kizzi's mama, and how he always loves
her. Talkin' like he's lookin' right at her. Sits up and calls out to
her . . . 'Venus.' Clear as day it was."

"Sallie, I don't understand. Who was Kizzi's mama? Was she
one of my parent's friends? God forbid she was a woman from a
brothel." Aware of rambling, Teresa Anne stopped talking.

"No, Madam. Old Lillian says she be youse daddy's slave. She
died in childbirth . . . birthin' Kizzi."

Repulsed and trying to avoid the reality of what she'd just
heard, Teresa Anne asked, "And who is old Lillian?"

"Old Lillian beens here since the beginnin' of time—old as
dirt—so she says. I reckon she here when Kizzi born. She don't
doos much now . . . can't hardly see or walk no more. The others
lookin' after her like she lookin' after them in past times."

"This is a lot to take in," Teresa Anne remarked. Swallowing
and pausing for a moment, she commented but barely above a whisper, "I must have a half-sister, and she's half . . . half . . . white. It

was impossible to say it differently. I have no right to ask, but Sallie would you please keep my daddy's dying words secret?"

"No one knows ceptin' youse. Umm, maybes old Lillian doos. Honey, there's lots of 'em in slave times . . . lighter they was."

"Promise you won't tell . . . in God's name."

"I's promise," she answered.

"Sallie, why wouldn't I know about Kizzie if she was in the house?"

"I can't say to that," she answered with a quick shake of her head.

"Do you know where Kizzi is now?"

"No, Madam. I doos not. Old Lillian says she comes back now and then. Says she sees her from time to time."

"Hum . . . did my daddy say where she went or why she left?"

"No, but youse daddy says Mistress knows. Old Lillian says she near to havin' a baby when she up and leaves. Don't reckon youse can rightly ask youse mama now a days. Ain't many round here no more hears of Kizzi. You can talk to Old Lillian, but I'm thinkin' cuz it's youse; she won't remember nothin'."

"Thank you Sallie. I'm glad we had this talk. I know I can depend on you to tend to my mama and to keep my daddy's words secret . . . both very important to me. You can go now."

"Yes'm."

"And remember, if you have more questions or think of anything, just seek me out. But if it's about Kizzi, please be cautious, so others can't hear."

"Yes'm."

When Teresa Anne talked to Charles and he asked how the conversation went, she answered, "We had a good chat. Thankfully, Sallie agreed to be the house supervisor." Without asking exactly what was discussed, he commented, "Excellent. Now we can leave this place. I mean, we can now go home and see Ethan."

"I'm going to sit with my mother for awhile. What are your plans?" Teresa Anne asked.

"I think I'll see to the carriage and tell Jefferson of our plans to leave early in the morning."

"Thank you Charles."

"For what my dear?"

"For your help and support."

"Can I have a kiss?" he asked with a smile on his face and a gleam in his eye.

Looking around to make sure no one was watching, Teresa Anne gave him a quick peck on the lips. Charles smiled but said, "Surely my help and support should bank me a better kiss."

After a much longer kiss—thinking it bordered on improper— Teresa Anne pulled away before remarking, "I want to go home too, but while here I must be a dutiful daughter and see to my mother."

Climbing the stairs, Teresa Anne wondered what her mother knew. Was she aware of her husband's feelings for a slave? Did she know a child was born who was half his? Instantly, her mother's devastating words were replayed in her mind, "It's my fault" and "I'm damned." Walking down the hall, Teresa Anne questioned but not out loud . . . oh Mother, what did you do? Feeling an immediate chill come over her, she arrived in front of her mother's bedroom door. Yes, her mother knew.

Knocking, as she'd done each time before, she'd quit trying to understand why. Full of apprehension she gently but steadily opened the door and entered. Without glancing toward the bed, she asked, "Daisy, is my mama still staying quiet?"

With a nod and a more relaxed attitude, Daisy answered, "Thank you for the medicine. It is surely a miracle. She is back to the way she was before it gone."

Sitting down beside her mother's bed, Teresa Anne said, "Mama, it's me . . . Teresa Anne. Can you see me?"

Unexpectedly, her mother answered in a clear voice, "Yes, I can see you. The grey smoke is gone, but it's difficult to open my eyes." Without additional prodding, she continued, "I'm so tired of suffering. When will this torture end? Can you help me?"

Although Teresa Anne did not like what she was hearing, it was pure wonderment to see and hear her mama engaged in rational thoughts and using words which made sense. "Mama, I don't know what to do except make certain you have medicine to help you sleep. Tell me what I can do to give you peace."

"I've been cursed, but you know already," she answered matter-of-factly.

"Mama, don't say such things. That's a bunch of make-believe."

"Teresa Anne, don't talk to me as William does. If you don't believe me; then you can't help me."

Not wanting to lose the best communication they'd had in a long time . . . fearing she'd return to silence or babbling, Teresa Anne offered, "What if I said I believe you? What could I do then?"

"You can help me pray for salvation, and then . . . push me out the window."

Hearing Daisy gasp—having forgotten she was still in the room—Teresa Anne turned in the servant's direction, "My mama seems clear in the head and still has on the ties to hold her down. Could you leave us alone for a few minutes? You can return when I leave the room."

It was as if her mother was not aware of her discussion with Daisy for she continued to talk in the background. Teresa Anne heard her say, "I tried to jump out the window, but she wouldn't get out of my way."

"Mama, I could never throw you out the window or harm you, but I can pray with you. You can also pray directly to God yourself. You don't need me to help you pray for salvation."

"When I try, she gets in the way."

"Who Mama? Who gets in the way? Tell me."

"Kizzi."

"Mama, please tell me about Kizzi. Then, I'll pray with you," Teresa Anne answered.

"Kizzi was a whore . . . just like her mama." After speaking those harsh words, her mother began to drool.

Promising herself to remain calm, Teresa Anne replied, "Let's have a little bit of medicine to calm you—not enough to put you to sleep—but enough so we can talk. Surprisingly, her mother welcomed the opium . . . opening her cracked lips and eagerly swallowing it.

Waiting for a few minutes and talking about mundane things, Teresa Anne said, "Mama, you know how much I love you. More than anything else, I want you to find peace. Why don't you just tell me what happened. I promise not judge you. Your fate will be between you and our Lord. And Mama, no matter what you say, I promise to pray with you afterwards. We both were taught that Jesus will forgive us if we repent and truly mean it." Even though her mama was presently clear-headed, Teresa Anne felt nothing good could be gained from sharing Daddy's passing with her.

After speaking of redemption, Teresa Anne looked in the direction of heaven and said the Lord's Prayer to herself. Returning to focus on her mama, she saw that her squinted eyes had completely closed. "Mama . . . no, no, no . . . don't go to sleep," Teresa Anne begged. Shaking her shoulder, she somewhat roused before replying softly, "I'm safe for now."

"Mama, while you're safe, tell me the story of Kizzi and her mother. Remember how you told me stories before putting me to bed. Please tell me one last story. Please don't sleep yet. I beg of you."

And just like that—without additional prodding—Abigail asked, "If I do, will you pray with me after?"

"Of course but we must hurry while you feel safe."

"I knew," she began with a sigh, "that William bedded Kizzi's mother. He'd done others, but it was different with that one. Strutted around the plantation like a peacock, he did. She put him in a trance and drew him to her. He made all kinds of excuses, but I was on to him. I learned she was expecting a child. William never told me, but I had my ways. When the child was born, the slave died; I thought good riddance. William treated me like a fool. Telling me he couldn't sell a girl slave. She could help Matilda. I put up with it. I couldn't bear to let him know I knew what was going on, but it made me sick. When he brought her into the house, it made me angry. I can't say more; I'm too tired."

"Stay awake Mama. I promise to pray with you, but you must tell me the whole story. I think we're almost to the story's end. Please continue Mama." With no response Teresa Anne shook her again; amazingly she started to talk again. "I ignored the child the best I could. Matilda looked after her, but I knew William watched her from afar. It was Matilda's task to keep her away from you at all times. I demanded it."

"Then what Mama? What happened to Kizzi? Why is it you believe you're cursed?"

"I cannot say it out loud. There is no forgiveness for what I did."

"Mama, how bad can it be?"

"I want to sleep. I'm safe, so leave it be," she answered.

"Mama, I'm leaving tomorrow to go to my home. This might be our only chance to pray for your soul. You must continue for your own sake. Stay awake, Mama . . . please."

"If I do, will you promise to end my suffering?" her mother asked, looking directly at her. It was more about the direction of her mama's head than actually seeing her eyes.

While having no intention of harming her, Teresa Anne answered, "I'll do my best to help you. That . . . I promise."

"Ronald took advantage of Kizzi when drunk. She put him in a trance just like her mother did William. When her stomach started growing with Ronald's child, I couldn't allow our family name to be sullied. No use to seek William's help; he would have protected his daughter and grandchild. The whore was no longer a slave . . . no longer a possession, and had to be disposed of. So . . . I did. Simple as that. It had to be done to save us from ridicule. But now she won't let me be . . . haunts me unless I sleep. Sometimes, even when I sleep. I see her and other hideous things, but your father doesn't believe me. Ronald saw her. She spooked his horse, and the reason why he died. She killed my son; I'm sure of it."

"How do you know you see her? What do you see when you see her?" Teresa Anne asked, surprisingly more curious than angry about what she'd just heard. Strangely, it was like hearing a despicable story about another family.

"She flies around in something white . . . Ronald said it was a white nightgown. She can be anywhere . . . go anywhere. Teresa Anne, leave while you can and never return."

Teresa Anne's felt the hairs on her arm stand straight up. Full of emotions of disgust for her mother's actions and frightened beyond sensible thought, her imagined dream returned.

If she believed it to be true, would the belief somehow give credence to Kizzi's existence? Refusing to dwell on any of it now, she told her mother, "Let's pray for your forgiveness and hope Jesus listens."

Kneeling down next to the bed—feeling weak and light headed—Teresa Anne uttered out loud, "Please God, take pity on us. We are sinners who need forgiveness." Waiting for her mother to join in, she heard snoring sounds. But regardless and wanting to keep her promise, she continued to pray . . . asking over and over for her mama to find peace and forgiveness. Her last request was for God to keep she and Charles safe, praying their faith would sustain them until they were far from Willowland Manor. When finished, she realized her face was wet from weeping; the tears unknowingly flowing down her cheeks while she'd prayed.

Walking down the stairs, she wondered what Charles would think when she told him. No, better to wait until they were safely home to discuss it . . . if at all. It was all so shameful . . . unspeakable for anyone to do but for her mother to do . . . she couldn't find a word bad enough to describe her mother's actions.

Teresa Anne did not see her mother before she left. She had more or less told her goodbye in her mind when she left her room the previous evening.

Out the door and steps away from the carriage, Sallie asked if she could speak with her. Afraid it was perhaps about Kizzi and wanting to talk alone, they stepped momentarily into the parlor.

"Madam, I wasn't thinkin' good the day past. I's thinkin' of bein' a boss and Kizzi . . . memberin' the Massa's words and all bout Kizzi. When I's first talked to youse father, he asked me to tells youse somethin'. Youse father tells me when for sure war was a comin', the dressin' room changed to Matilda's sleepin' room. Space was put behind the wall to hide valuables. After the war, the valuables taken out to be displayed once more. Massa says only he, Mistress, and Matilda knows it be there but says you should knows. Says nothin's theres no more."

With relief and fearing she'd changed her mind, Teresa Anne said, "Thank you Sallie. I'll see to it when I come again."

"Haves a safe journey to youse home," Sallie answered but didn't smile. What was there to smile about? It wasn't her place to be in charge . . . she was just a lowly cook. But if Madam said so—like Massa—then her wishes would be followed. So be it.

# Chapter 20

Mississippi 2010

*W*as it a vision, a spirit, a ghost . . . what? At first frightened I began to wonder if I was going crazy. Sitting down and beginning to doubt myself, did I really see what I thought I saw? Maybe it was a combination of light coming through the window and the full glasses of wine before, during, and after dinner . . . and fear. My dad's words entered my mind, "Don't be a baby; the dark can't hurt you. It's your imagination that's the culprit."

On my travels up the Mississippi River from New Orleans to Memphis, I'd purposely booked several old hotels, finding them intriguing but didn't seek ones considered to be haunted. Although a list of such hotels existed, I considered their advertisements a bunch of hooey. Even though Dad would disagree, I wasn't into ridiculous stuff like he was. And, as I'd often told him, "Dad, since I deem myself a sane person; I don't believe in spiritual manifestations."

Tomorrow, I'll inquire if anyone else had any such . . . . Not knowing exactly what I'd seen, I questioned what to call it. I'll figure out how to approach the subject later, but for now all I wanted to do was go to sleep . . . if that was even possible. Since leaving tomorrow for my next stop, I should have started to pack earlier, but decided it could wait until after breakfast. Staying at Willowland Manor for only two days, there really wasn't much to pack . . . easily accomplished before the noon check-out time.

Still sitting on the bed, she retraced her steps after dinner, replaying the events leading up to the incident. She was staying alone on the second floor of the manor in a room not far from the main stairs. After getting ready for bed and pulling down the bedspread, she turned off the main light, reading by her battery book-light for awhile. Deciding to make a final bathroom stop, she quietly stepped out into the hall. Enjoying the ambiance of the old hotel—choosing this location for that very reason—she listened to the floor boards creak with each step and grinned. Walking slowly to the bathroom—another appeal of not having a modern private bathroom attached to her room—she tried to remember how old the hotel was, reminding herself to check the brochure again tomorrow. Returning from the old but functional bathroom, she entered the room without turning on the light, using the moonlight filtering through the window to guide her. Stopping in front of the window, she looked out at the willow trees in the near distance, marveling at how huge and beautiful they were. Wondering what time it was but deciding it really didn't matter, she turned toward the bed. Hearing a muffled swishing sound—which seemed to come from behind—or was it merely a feeling something wasn't quite right or someone was in the room. Regardless of what caught her attention, she turned back to see a shadowy woman coming through the door from the hall. Huh . . . through the closed door. How could it be possible . . . as entrance was impossible.

Knowing the door was both closed and locked, she stood there astonished; the hair on her arms sticking straight up. When she found her voice, having not considered speaking or moving until the figure eerily passed, she called out, "What are you doing in my room?" Even while asking, she knew how ridiculous she sounded. Without an answer, the vision quietly and somewhat mechanically moved toward the window, then melted away. Only seconds had passed, yet the feel of woolen material against her hand remained.

Glued to the floor and unable to grasp what had just happened, she stood there stunned and blinking her eyes. Logically, she could attribute the entire episode to the earlier glasses of wine. However, not feeling the least bit tipsy, this conclusion seemed a better choice than losing her marbles.

Intrigued and strangely no longer frightened, she pushed heavily upward against the window to open it, breaking a nail in the process. Thinking more about the disappearing person, vision, or whatever it was, she wanted to look out the open window for a closer look below . . . not sure why or for what reason. The encounter made no logical sense. In the back of her mind and regardless of how much she tried to disregard it, there was no denying something supernatural had just occurred. Turning on the overhead light and planning to leave it on the entire night, she returned to bed.

Waking early the following morning, her first thoughts were of the previous night's incident. Having a plan, she hurriedly dressed and left for breakfast. Fearing she'd be classed a fool; she looked around the dining room, trying to decide which employee to ask about her experience.

After seating a middle-aged couple by the window, the hostess—a lady probably in her thirties or early forties—walked by her table. Preparing to speak but bordering on embarrassment, she took a quick sip of coffee. The jagged nail on her index finger caught her attention . . . giving her the courage to say something.

"Pardon me. Are you at a place where you can stop and talk to me . . . just for a moment? I want to ask you a question."

"I'm on an errand but will be right back. If you're still here, I can sit a spell."

"Thank you. I'll wait."

Within five minutes, the hostess returned, saying, "What can I do for you?"

"Would you mind to sit down? What I'm going to ask will probably sound silly."

Her answer was surprising, "I doubt if anything you could ask or tell me would sound silly. Honey, I've heard it all."

"I'm not sure how to ask but here goes. I had a rather bazaar experience—both shocking and frightening—last night in my room."

With no signs of surprise and in a matter-of-fact manner she replied, "Go on."

"I saw a woman in my room. She was like a vision you read about in ghost stories. She was dressed in black with a black veil. When she brushed against my hand, the material felt like wool."

When I finished saying my spill, I looked closely at her for some reaction, but there was none. Without an answer and not what I expected for such an unusual admission—I asked almost apologetically, "Has anyone else seen this person or had a similar experience?

I'm so confused by it." Beginning to feel self conscious, I quickly added, "Maybe it was a nightmare or my imagination." When she smiled, I wasn't exactly sure what to make of her facial expression. Did she think what I said was funny? Did she think what I saw was funny?

After a seemingly thoughtful pause, she asked, "Did you happen to see the portrait in the parlor?" Not waiting for my response, she continued, "It is said to be the daughter of the original builder and owner of the manor. She's painted in a black outfit and veil . . . supposedly done after losing her third son to a riding accident."

"I haven't seen the portrait so don't think that's a possibility. In fact I haven't been in the parlor before." After responding, it crossed my mind to question why someone would want a portrait done in mourning attire. Perhaps it was a custom done back in those days.

"Well, to be honest others have mentioned similar sightings. We don't usually discuss it. Management feels it might frighten people away. Myself, I think it would bring in more business. But what do I know. No one asks my opinion," she finished with a shrug.

"Thank you for taking the time to talk to me. Before I leave today, I'll make a point to go into the parlor to see the portrait, especially while the vision is still fresh on my mind. I'm fascinated by old buildings. After rechecking this morning, it's hard to believe Willowland Manor was built in 1815."

"Yeah, that's a long time ago . . . isn't it? From what I've been told, it's gone through many owners and lots of renovations since then. If I don't see you again before you leave, thanks for staying with us at Willowland. Honey, I hope you'll come back."

All the while knowing she should be upstairs packing, she was drawn to the parlor to look for the portrait. Casually entering and wondering why she'd not checked the room out sooner; it was an extraordinary sitting area. Memorabilia of the hotel, old pictures, newspaper articles, and portraits were abundant everywhere. Some of the furniture appeared to be the same ones displayed in newspaper articles from past years. Working her way across the walls, her eyes finally settled on the lady in black with the black veil. Below was a name plate: Abigail Hattin Wayland. Unlike her vision, the veil did not completely cover her face—more like hanging down each side. The face wasn't recognizable, but then she didn't remember seeing a face last night so had nothing to compare it to. Besides, it happened so quickly, yet the outfit and body structure seemed identical to her vision. Damn, that seemed weird, but was proof the encounter was not only believable but also fact. So . . . now what? Having credible proof in her mind of the event didn't mean others would believe her. Would she believe a person talking about seeing a ghost? No, she wouldn't. Would she consider such a person rational? No, she wouldn't. How can something be explained, yet be unexplainable? One thing for sure . . . a person who lived many years ago became visible to her last night, and she found what happened to be far beyond rational understanding. However, her father would have no problem believing what she saw—without reservation—but then, he was into such stuff.

On a whim, she stopped by the front desk, asking if perhaps she could stay a couple of more days . . . maybe today and tomorrow.

"Yes, of course . . . that's no problem. We're not booked, and you can remain in the same room, if you like, or move to another after the sighting."

"So, I guess the hostess told you. I'm kinda embarrassed about it."

"Don't be. Lots of guests have seen apparitions here. It's part of our mystique," she replied with a friendly giggle.

"Well, it's my first encounter . . . ever. It was both frightening and fascinating. I'm curious to see if it happens again tonight. Has anyone been harmed by . . . ?"

"No, just sightings . . . some more fascinating than others."

"Like what? What have they seen? More than a woman in black clothing?"

"I'm sorry, but I need to get back to work. Lots to do," she answered and smiled.

While saying, "Thank you for changing my reservation," the lady hadn't seemed busy. In fact she'd looked bored and might have been doodling when she first stopped there. When she turned to leave, she noticed a frowning gentleman standing in the doorway behind the desk counter.

Now, more intrigued than ever, how much could she learn about Abigail Hattin Wayland and perhaps others in the next two days? Going to her room to cancel her next hotel reservation, she needed to devise a new plan. What would her next step be in proving the impossible? She was not only enjoying herself, but it seemed like a legitimist purpose for staying there, and one her dad would actually approve of.

Finishing her phone call, she started with the assumption that the portrait and the unexplainable presence were the same. So . . .

why appear to her? It was a true mystery, and one she'd do her best to solve before leaving. Okay, what would Dad do first? Knowing he would concentrate on why Abigail Wayland was still wandering through Willowland Manor after so many years, she should gather as much information on her as possible. That was pretty much a given, she thought, and definitely what Dad would expect her to do. Get the facts first . . . speculate later . . . he'd say. She wanted to call him but decided to investigate more before surprising him with her latest news.

Since Willowland Manor was originally a plantation built during pre-civil war days, there should be a family graveyard on the land . . . normally close to the main house; which was now the hotel. If such a burial ground still existed, would management allow her to visit it?

Returning to the reservation desk, she inquired, "Excuse me. Is there a family burial plot near the hotel, and if so, could I check it out?"

Without specifically answering her question the same lady from before said, "Give me a moment, and I'll ask."

She disappeared through the same narrow door where the man was standing before. After a minute or so, she returned, and said, "I'm sorry but due to liability issues, the manager said it would be impossible to give you permission to go there."

"So I take it a family graveyard does exist," thinking she'd wander around and find it on her own. Without a reply she continued, "Perhaps an employee can take me to see it." Then, with a straight face she quickly added an out-and-out lie, "I'm doing research for a magazine on Southern plantations converted into hotels."

"Let me see," she answered, this time seemingly more interested.

Returning quickly, she said, "The manager will be out to talk with you."

"Thank you," was uttered but thought . . . how about that, a little lie getting the job done.

"Just have a seat; he shouldn't be long," the desk clerk replied with another smile.

"Thank you so much. I'll be right back. I need to go to my room to get a notebook and my camera."

Rushing upstairs, she'd barely returned to the lobby when a gentleman—the man she expected to see—introduced himself. When he asked what magazine she represented, she answered vaguely, "I'm on assignment but would rather not say at this time. If your hotel is included, then you'll receive paperwork and release forms." As she spoke, she wondered if he'd been told about her experience from the previous night. Probably so.

She followed him outside and around to the side of the building. From there they exited through a rickety wooden gate; its paint noticeably flecking off. Walking along an unkempt pathway, they approached an uneven rock fence, barely visible through tall weeds and thick bushes. Entering a break in the fence, mindful of the rough and protruding branches, she found herself amongst a multitude of scattered gravesites. In the approximate center of the graveyard was one large gravestone with many smaller ones surrounding it. At first it was difficult to see where they were separated, but as she got closer, it became somewhat easier. Most of the smaller headstones were either hidden by weeds, sunken in the dirt, or covered with moss. A few of the gravesites had ruminants of wooden markers; many were unmarked.

Trying to engage the gentleman in conversation, she asked, "Have you been here often?"

"No, I don't like graveyards. They give me the creeps," he answered curtly.

"If you don't mind, I'm going to stay awhile and take notes and pictures. I'll be fine if you want to leave. I'm especially curious about the oldest section. Where do you think that is?"

"Can't help you with that," he answered matter-of-factly.

Well, so much for being helpful with the magazine article, she thought sarcastically. "I love to visit old cemeteries. I find them interesting. They hold so much history." Without receiving comment, she watched him move near the entrance and stop. He appeared perturbed but did not leave.

Starting with the biggest tombstone—usually considered the most important occupant in a cemetery—she could easily read the large lettering: HATTIN. Knowing the camera would pick up some but not all of the other faded information, she began writing down as much as she could read. Below the main name and still fairly clear: Rustice Bligh (on one side) Margaret Clever (on the other). Below their names: Father and Mother but the smaller dates of their births and deaths were unreadable.

Glancing to the front and both sides of the Hattin headstone, there were a mismatch of various size gravesites: some with tombstones, some enclosed by large rocks with no markers, some with wooden markers only, and some totally unmarked. Feeling a tad disrespectful, she gingerly stepped through the nearest graves to the Hattin sight. Thinking it odd, the closest grave was marked with a large wooden cross. Although weathered, she could still make out the letter W for the first name and the letter W for the last name. She assumed the last name's W stood for Wayland. It looked as though the letters were originally carved and then burned into the wood. The next grave over had a stone marker with the name Abigail Hattin Wayland. She felt like jumping with joy, but had the good sense to remain calm. The year of her birth was impossible to read but the year of her death was 1880. Quickly calculating, that would be one hundred and thirty years ago. Simply amazing, she thought. Directly below those gravesites were three grave areas, separated by rocks. Each had a small headstone but the lettering on them was impossible to read. Taking more pictures of the over-all graveyard—just in case they would be incorporated into her imaginary magazine article—she felt as if she'd already made progress. The most important learned fact; the lady in black was buried there.

Before thanking the manager for his helpfulness, she thought about telling him the graveyard should be tended to . . . giving the deceased the respect they deserved but decided not to say anything negative. For sure she didn't feel the least bit guilty for lying to him. On the contrary she felt elated by the ease of using the magazine ruse to acquire information. If necessary, she planned on using it again in the future. Besides, pretending to be an investigative reporter gave her purpose and seemed to take away some of the self-doubting account of the figure appearing in her room. Again, why her and why that particular room? Then it struck her. Was she somehow opening a can of worms by delving into the unknown? Thinking, she'd make sure her door was locked before retiring. Wanting to laugh at herself . . . yeah right, like locking the door would make a difference. Did she wish for another visit? Yes, if she didn't get hurt or God forbid . . . scared to death.

It wasn't like she hadn't been acquainted through the years with the occult and ghost stories. Growing up with her college professor father, she'd been surrounded by those associated with his paranormal investigative classes. He called it Parapsychology and had been outwardly disappointed in her lack of interest. She knew Dad would be jealous because she'd actually experienced what he'd been looking for his entire life. Spending the bulk of his time debunking ghost encounters, she looked forward to telling him she'd seen a ghost in the flesh . . . so to speak and wanted to laugh. Still, if anyone could give her insight into what happened last night, he could.

Having not talked to her parents in at least two months, it was definitely past time to give them a call. Not only a good time to connect with them but get her father's opinion on her experience. Let's see, what time would it be in Seattle? Looking at her watch— almost eleven in the morning— two hours earlier there—so he'd already be at work. Okay, she'd do more investigating and call him this evening.

While having lunch in the dining room and hoping for additional information, she looked for the out-going hostess but didn't see her. After diagramming the center of the graveyard—concentrating on the graves closest to the largest tombstone—she wanted to add names or perhaps juicy stories about the deceased lying there. For sure she'd revisit the parlor again for more connections to the family cemetery.

Finishing lunch, she sought out the clerk again. "Hi, I'm sorry to bother you again, but I have a couple of questions. Your brochure says this hotel is registered with the Mississippi Historical Society. Do you know where information like that is kept or where I can fine more information on the Hattin and Wayland family histories?

"Let me think. Probably in the state capitol. I'll look in our phone book for you."

While watching her flip through the pages, she wished she could use her laptop to look it up in seconds, but that was another appeal to this hotel . . . no internet connection.

"Yes, looks like it's in Jackson, but there's a local historical group in Vicksburg. Do you want both telephone numbers?"

"That would be great. Thank you so much," answered with true appreciation.

The rest of the day came and went with little progress. She tried the two phone numbers but received answering machine messages at both of them. She didn't leave a call-back number, deciding to first talk with Dad about pertinent questions to ask. She did visit the parlor and sneak back to the graveyard, hoping to find something missed earlier but to no avail.

During dinner, the woman—part of the couple seated by the window at breakfast—bounded over to her table and asked, "Are you the person who saw a ghost in your room?"

Totally caught off-guard, she asked back, "Where did you hear that?"

"The hostess told us. To be fair I asked her if there had been any new sightings since my cousin was here a year ago. Isn't this just the greatest place to stay?"

"Yes, it is. This is my first time to stay here. How about you?"

"Oh no, we stay here at least once a year. I keep hoping to see something but never do."

"But your cousin did?" I asked casually, wanting to know if a person dressed in black appeared.

"Yes, he saw two confederate soldiers walking along the upstairs hall. I guess they walked right through him. He said it was the weirdest experience he'd ever had. Is that what you saw?

"No, I saw a lady dressed in black."

"Really! I've been coming here for years and haven't heard of that one."

"So, have you heard of others?" she asked curiously.

"Just one other. Two years ago, an older gentleman was sitting in the parlor and dozed off. He said when he awoke in the dark-ened room, a young man walked right past him . . . walking with only one leg. Knowing the impossibility of this occurring—both the ghost and walking without two legs—he checked out the next morning. I wouldn't have known about it except we were checking in when he was leaving. They kept asking him to keep his voice down." Smiling, she continued, "Of course it only made me want to listen more."

# Chapter 21

Finishing dinner without further interesting conversation, she called her father. He answered, "Hello," as if interrupted before following with, "Whatever you're selling; I'm not buying."

"Dad, it's Samantha. You sound angry."

"Those damn telemarketers. Can't get rid of them . . . it's day and night. Where are you this time?"

"I'm in Mississippi."

"Why Mississippi?" he asked with an air of surprise.

"I'm checking out old hotels."

"Aren't you ever going to settle down like a real person?" he asked bluntly.

Expecting his question, she responded quickly, "Maybe someday . . . when I'm ready."

"Your mom and I have given up on that ever happening. Are you doing all right money wise?"

"You know me; I work long enough to get-by until my next adventure."

"I don't know what to say. We do wish you were like your brothers—working regular jobs and leading productive lives."

"Dad, I didn't call to get lecture 101. Actually, I have something exciting to tell you and then ask some questions. Is this a good time?"

"Sure, but I only lecture—if that's what you want to call it— because we worry about you."

"I know, but here's the deal. I'm staying at a really old hotel on the Mississippi River about halfway between Vicksburg and Natchez. Last night, a figure—dressed in black with a black veil covering her face—passed by me in my closed and locked hotel room. She then disappeared into a window on the opposite side of the room."

"Interesting," was his only comment.

"Wait . . . there's more. The same person's portrait is in the parlor, and even better, the name under the portrait is the same as on a tombstone in the family graveyard. Her gravesite is near the hotel . . . once the mansion on the cotton plantation."

This time, he answered with true curiosity, "Very interesting."

"Even though you teach this stuff, have you ever had an experience like this before?"

"Definitely not. You're not taking any weird drugs . . . are you?"

"Dad, really? I'm talking about real stuff here. Wait, I've written down some questions." Not waiting for his response to possibly take her off-track, she began her bombardment. "Why me? Why the room where I'm staying? Do spirits choose who they show themselves to? It's been one hundred and thirty years since her death, so why is she still here? What should I do next?"

"Slow down. First things first. Now ask me again but slower and give me time to respond," he calmly replied.

Starting at the top of the list, she asked again, "Why me?"

"I doubt it has anything to do with you personally. Perhaps you are staying in her former bedroom. Probably there's a reason why she disappeared into the window. She might have been looking for something or someone."

"Okay, you've taken care of number one and also number two. From what you've gathered through the years, what's your opinion on why she's still here?"

"What happened to your third question? I jotted them down as quickly as I could . . . something about choosing who they manifest to."

"Oh yeah, I skipped it. So tell me, do they?"

"I'm not sure. That's a hard one to answer. She didn't seem to be seeking out your assistance. It is thought earthbound entities stay where they're comfortable or close to the familiar. I'm thinking you just happened to be in the right place at the right time and near her objective or where she wanted to go at that particular place and time."

"So Dad, how does one figure out why she's still hanging around after such a long period of time?"

"Without any of the facts, it's difficult to say. Perhaps she hasn't found peace after the death of her physical body. Sometimes, a spirit might be stuck in this world because they have unfinished business or don't realize they're dead. Some are caught in an unforgiveable limbo state due to a hellish event they caused. Say . . .

like the spirit of a murderer who dies in prison and wanders aimlessly within the prison walls . . . often seen by others through the years. Your lady in black might be connected to the land or held to the plantation because she was unable to fix a problem she caused when alive. It's also possible something happened quickly . . . say, like death by gunshot, causing a ghost to wander in a familiar place because they can't accept the finality of their death. I've heard of many earthbound soldiers wandering endlessly. Usually, military death records are easily found but not in this instance. It's hard to speculate without more information. Doing research can help but records may not be available for that far back. You might find dates but not the reason for the passing, especially for a person who wasn't famous." Taking a deep breath, he jokingly added, "Now you've heard lecture 101."

"Well, I'm off to Vicksburg tomorrow to see if I can locate more information on her and her family. I have her mother and father's names and her married name. That should give me a starting spot . . . don't you think? If there's nothing on them in Vicksburg, I'm going to the Mississippi state capital . . . Jackson. They're bound to have more records there. What else do you suggest I do?"

"Samantha, I must say I'm very impressed by your diligence. You seemed to have a handle on it. It appears something I said rubbed off on you after all."

"You don't know the half of it. I've gotten pretty creative in my quest for answers."

"Good for you. Keep me informed about your progress and let me know if I can help further."

"Thanks Dad. Tell Mom I said, 'Hi' and will call again soon. Wait . . . is Mom there? I'll tell her myself."

"No, she's next door."

"Okay, I'll call soon. I promise."

"We'll look forward to hearing from you," he replied sincerely.

"Bye, Dad."

"Bye, Samantha."

After deciding there was nothing more to learn at Willowland Manor, she changed her reservation again, wanting to leave the following day in the morning. Even though keyed-up, she went to bed unusually early, waiting for a visit, or sighting, or something odd to occur. Disappointed, nothing happened except a lot of tossing and turning throughout the night.

Although not sleeping well and beginning the day feeling tired, she was packed and checked-out by 10:30 AM. Having read about the history surrounding Vicksburg before leaving New Orleans, she was looking forward to her stay at another antebellum hotel. The hotel would be a jumping off spot to various Civil War battlefields and museums. Even as she thought about her original plan to explore the Vicksburg area, her new priority had changed to learning more about Abigail Hattin Wayland and the family members who'd lived at Willowland Manor.

# Chapter 22

The Present

*S*itting behind his desk, Matthew closed his eyes and massaged his temples. He knew before taking the phone call it would be trouble. His secretary knew it too. She paused and swallowed before saying in an apologetic manner, "You have a call from George, ah . . . from the Mississippi project on line two."

Picking up the receiver and pushing the blinking button, he sighed and asked, "Now what . . . tell me something good."

"Wish I could. You'll need to handle this one personally."

As Matthew listened, he knew this new situation had the possibility of delaying the entire project's finish but calmly told him, "George, with a little luck we might get through this latest hiccup unscathed. I'll be back there on Monday." Realistically thinking, we could actually be okay if the involved parties cooperate quickly. Since the Grand Opening Ceremony was scheduled in less than three months, he couldn't let anything or anybody jeopardize the opening . . . or his job.

Problem after problem with the Mississippi acquisition was finally wearing him down. Every time he thought they were back on schedule, a major hurdle rose up to bite him in the ass. He'd promised the investment group's CEO he'd deliver the project on time and on budget. The response he'd received was direct an unequivocal, "You better or you're gone."

Most of the problems encountered had been beyond his control. But it really didn't matter when it came to the bottom line. Either he produced or he was history with this endeavor and most likely any future ones. He reminded himself of that fact every morning before work and thought about it each night before going to bed. If this job worked out, he could pretty much name his price for future undertakings. If not, his whole life would change and not for the better. After what he'd put his family through while away, if the project ended up late or in the red, he doubted his wife would stick with him a single day longer.

He pushed the intercom button and asked his secretary to return to his office. "Betty, please make the usual flight plans, rent the usual car, and etcetera. You know the drill. Plan for an early flight Monday . . . no need to rush there on the weekend. The people I need to talk to won't be available until Tuesday."

"Are you all right?" she asked.

"I'm just tired of the constant obstructions. I should have moved my family back there four years ago when this started. I just didn't anticipate . . . . Sorry, not your concern."

"Is that all?" she inquired politely.

"Yes, thank you. After you set up the arrangements, take off and have a good weekend."

"You too," she answered. Before leaving, she questioned, "Will you come in Monday or leave from home?"

"Home makes more sense. Thank you. See you when I return . . . hopefully sooner than later."

While certain he'd find what he was after, Matthew removed a thick file folder from his briefcase and flipped through it. He'd lost track of most of the paperwork but knew it was either in his brief-case or somewhere in a file cabinet in his office. Since the begin-ning, four years had passed—four long and tedious years—along with the accompanying magnitude of papers, copies, and diagrams.

When originally hired, he was just an assistant project manager . . . one of five employed for their areas of expertise. His was overseeing the building of the new clubhouse on the golf course.

Not involved with the early stages of the project, those matters had been handled by the financial and legal departments before he came onboard. The design of the golf course was done with input from named pro golfers, so his job was to work with the building contractor and the design committee to make sure the clubhouse was built according to the blueprints, permits, and satisfied the wishes of the Board of Trustees and investors.

After the sudden death of the Project Manager—who the assistant managers answered to—each assistant was called in to give their vision for completing the entire project. Since the assistants had already gone through the vetting process, if the review board didn't hear what they were looking for, they would go outside to find someone else . . . even though the project was well on its way by then. After extensive meet-ings, the board agreed with his plan to proceed, ultimately promoting him to Project Manager. At the time he felt being chosen had a lot to do with how he'd taken care of the consequences of a terrible storm which flooded most of the golf course and some of the accompany-ing building sites. Luckily, he'd been on site, minimizing the damage and saving massive amounts of building materials and diverting flood waters away from prime areas. It had been a hectic time but he'd been openly praised and appreciated by the higher-ups.

Being promoted was wonderful news for his career but created a personal family conflict. He was needed in Mississippi every week until the project was finished . . . basically for four years. It meant he would be responsible to oversee the renovation of an old hotel already on the property, the building of a new hotel, the golf course, the clubhouse, and the paddleboat casino to be docked close-by on the Mississippi River. Hoping to depend heavily on his assistants, he realized early-on and to do it right, the project needed hands-on direction almost daily.

After hearing about this latest problem, he shuttered at telling his wife, Brooke, of the necessity for him to be off to Mississippi again . . . after being gone for two weeks straight and only home for a mere two days.

Locating the information he wanted to check out, he placed it back inside the folder, closed his briefcase, and locked it. Looking around the office, he picked up his suit jacket and quietly left.

During the drive home he kept going over what to say to Brooke. Some of the words he thought about using—but shouldn't—were the same ones he'd used many times before. He remembered how excited he'd been when telling her about landing the new position and the great salary which came with it. "Brooke, think about what this means for us?" Her response wasn't what he expected and a real ego deflator. "I hope you don't expect me to quit my job and move to Mississippi. Definitely, you can't expect to take Ashlynn out of school. She's barely coping with going to high school as it is. She'll be devastated to leave her friends."

"Honey, I'll make it work somehow," he'd told her back then but was disappointed when she'd not shared in his elation. In the back of his mind, he'd thought he'd win her over to his way of thinking. In the beginning they e-mailed constantly, talked on the phone about what was going on in their lives, and generally enjoyed their time when back together again in New Jersey . . . if only for a few days. However, the phone calls became less frequent and the e-mails were all about how she had to handle everything at home on her own . . . even the problems associated with Ashlynn. When he offered advice, she became defensive and told him, "You're not here, so what do you know?" As time passed, she had her life in New Jersey and he had his in Mississippi.

When he tried to share a problem at work or even an accomplishment, she showed little interest. He'd finally asked if she was having an affair. She answered promptly as though she'd been considering it, "No, but I should. We sure don't have a marriage anymore."

As he left for work this morning, his wife's parting remark, "This better be over soon—as promised—or our marriage is over." How could he defend himself? He knew she felt as if she was raising Ashlynn alone, watching their daughter become more introverted with each passing day. It didn't help discovering Ashlynn's latest problem—cutting herself. Brooke needed to take off work to drive their daughter to her weekly therapy sessions. When he asked the reason for the new cutting development, she remarked, "What do you care?" When he asked Ashlynn to help him understand what was going on, she denied anything was wrong before saying, "It's been accidental; Mom's just over-reacting." He knew it wasn't accidental, but what could he say . . . call his daughter a liar.

Maybe it would be better to tell Brooke he wanted to stay in Mississippi fulltime, because he was treated better there by strangers . . . not mentioning anything about the new problem which could delay the opening of the Willowland Resort. He was tired of being treated like the bad guy. All he ever wanted to do was give his family security . . . something he'd never had while growing up. That was neither here nor there. Brooke knew he grew up extremely poor.

Almost home, he came up with what he thought was a brilliant idea. School was out for the summer, so perhaps the family could go to Mississippi together. If he could talk Brooke into it, it would be a chance for the family to mend and get back on track.

When he arrived home, Ashlynn was in her room with the light off. Knocking briefly on the half-open door, he said, "Hi Kiddo. What's with the light being off?"

"I don't know. I didn't realize it had gotten dark outside."

"Where's Mom? I thought she'd be home by now."

"She called, and said she was going out to Happy Hour with people from work."

"Did she say where?"

"Nope."

"Are you hungry?" he asked, trying not to show how upset he felt.

"Not really," she replied.

"How about we go out and misbehave and have something decadent to eat."

"That would make Mom mad," she answered quietly.

"Why?"

"She doesn't want me to get fat."

"What harm can one meal make? You look too thin to me anyway. Besides, she doesn't need to know."

"She'll find out. She watches everything I do or eat."

"She'll get over it. I'll tell her I made you go."

Perking up, Ashlynn asked, "Can I have French fries?"

"Absolutely."

Watching his daughter grab her purse, he realized how much he'd missed while chasing his dream. Maybe he'd done all of this to prove something to himself. Perhaps Brooke was right. He'd put the job before his wife and family. But it had been Brooke's choice to stay and not follow him to Mississippi. She didn't need to work, and they could have found a similar private school for Ashlynn. So it wasn't completely his fault, he reasoned.

They sat at a local hamburger hang out and talked about Ashlynn's plans for the immediate future while out of school. Deciding to broach the Mississippi trip before discussing it with his wife, he asked, "Would you like to see what Dad's been doing in Mississippi?"

"Yeah, that would be cool," she answered.

"I haven't discussed it with your mom yet, so I'm not sure what her vacation plans are like."

"She talked to me about it, but it was going to be a surprise. I shouldn't say."

He saw her swirl a French fry in catsup and then slowly savor it. Trying to remember the last time just the two of them had been out to dinner, he remarked, "This is fun . . . isn't it?"

"It is . . . lots." Cocking her head, she seriously asked, "You promise not to say anything to Mom about the fries . . . right?"

"Right. I'm ordering two sundaes. What flavor do you want? I'm having a strawberry with nuts on top."

"I better not. After half a hamburger and fries, I don't think I have room."

"How about this. Order your favorite and if you can't finish it, I will. Is that a deal?"

After ordering her chocolate sundae with bananas, he asked for the bill. Then asked, "How is life treating you? Talk to me."

"About what?" she asked with a frown.

"Tell me about your therapy sessions, and if they're helping."

"I'm not supposed to discuss it . . . not even with Mom. It makes her mad when I tell her that."

"Really. Doesn't Mom talk to the therapist?"

"I guess so," she answered uncomfortably

"I can relate to your mom getting mad. I'm not her favorite person right now either. She gets mad about what I say or don't say, so I hear ya."

Speaking up, Ashlynn started to volunteer information. "When I try to tell Mom something, she tells me I'm talking nonsense or being ridiculous. I've just stopped telling her anything."

"Like what? I'm a good listener and promise not to say anything like that."

"I'd rather not say. You'll think I'm ridiculous too."

"Give me a try and then I'll tell you some things I haven't even told your mom. That seems fair . . . doesn't it?"

"Okay, but don't tell Mom I said anything."

"You have my word," he answered, hoping what she told him wouldn't be so awful that he could keep his word.

With her head down and whispering his daughter was difficult to hear, so he scooted closer. "I feel ugly and hate my hair. I don't know how to act around boys, cuz they don't like me."

Waiting to make sure she'd finished, Matthew smiled before saying, "I can't believe it; my sister said those exact words to me a long time ago. It was during her freshman year in high school. I was a senior."

"What did you say back to her?" she asked, speaking up and fully engaged in the conversation.

"I told her what seems important now will hardly be remembered later. You know your Aunt Janice is married to a great guy and has four kids. She called me not too long ago and reminded me about our conversation, and how she now realized all girls think there is something wrong with the way they look. Either they're too skinny or too fat, too tall or too short, or it's something else. One of her daughters is having similar feelings, and she told her how some girls are able to cover up those feelings better than others. She also told her daughter what her Uncle Matt said to her when she had those same doubts in high school."

"Dad, are you telling me this for reals?"

"Yes, I am . . . for reals."

"Thanks Dad."

"For what?"

"You know."

"Not really but you're welcome."

"Dad, let's go home and ask Mom about going to Mississippi."

"Okay, let's do it."

Arriving home, Matthew could hear noise coming from the kitchen. Ashlynn entered first and he followed. Brooke looked toward the door, saying, "Hi Ashie," and ignored him.

Doing his best to sound up-beat and not acknowledge the lack of being addressed, he said, "Hi, Honey."

"Good evening," she replied in a reserved manner. Followed by a sarcastic, "Thanks for leaving me a note."

"Well, thanks for letting me know where you were," he answered just as sarcastically.

"I told Ashlynn," she quipped.

"I said, thanks for letting 'me' know."

"Who'd think you'd be home from your precious job before me," she answered.

Ashlynn interrupted their back-and-forth by saying, "Mom, Dad wants to ask you something."

"What now?" she asked with a shrug.

"How about the three of us sit and talk a minute," Matthew offered.

"I'm heating some soup. Anyone want to join me or did you already eat?"

Dodging the next anticipated questions for Ashlynn's sake— like where did you go and what did you eat—he replied, "We did eat but will sit with you anyway." Waiting for her to get settled,

Matthew began. "Before you answer or get angry, I'd like for you and Ashlynn to go back to Mississippi with me. I'd really like to show you both around. It's turned into a beautiful place in a lovely location." Looking directly at Brooke, he added, "I'm proud to be a part of it and would like you to see it. Can you take vacation time off?"

"Are you talking about right now? If so, that's impossible."

As soon as her mom said the word "impossible" Ashlynn pushed back from the table and scurried out of the room.

"Yes, right now. Wouldn't it be fun for us as a family? There's also a lot of history in that part of the South. You've never been there, and it would be a great adventure for Ashlynn."

"Now won't work for me. Others in my department are already out on vacation. I've put in for my vacation for a later time. I was going to surprise you at the Grand Opening. That's when I requested my full month off."

"Wow, I had no idea. That's really great. So, how about Ashlynn coming with me for a week or so?"

"I'll need to think about it. I know she'll be bored here at home with school out of session." As if thinking out loud, she continued. "I'll need to cancel her therapy sessions. See if the therapist is all right with her leaving."

"Brooke, she'll be fine with me. I'll keep her busy. She can actually help with something I'll be working on . . . research stuff. So, you're really coming to the Grand Opening. That blows me away . . . as Ashlynn would say."

"That's the plan," she answered without the previous edge in her voice.

As if a decision had been made, Matthew stood and hollered for Ashlynn to come back. Thinking he'd need to look for her reading in her room, she suddenly appeared. "Ashlynn, your mother said it would be okay for you to go with me to Mississippi. This is going to be fun. I'll call my secretary to add another plane ticket."

After squealing, "Whoopee," Ashlynn gave them each a kiss and rushed off to her room.

When certain Ashlynn couldn't hear, Brook offered, "Thank you for saying I said it was okay. I'm not a very popular person as far as Ashlynn is concerned . . . maybe not to anyone in this house. When are you talking about leaving?"

Brooke's "not to anyone" remark duly noted; Matthew answered, "Monday," but didn't look her way.

"That soon? No way can she be ready by then."

"Sure she can. If she forgets something, I'll buy it for her."

"Matthew, we're talking just two days. How long will she be gone?"

"I'm thinking she'll come back with me in a week. If she's having fun and likes the adventure, she can return with me again. I really do miss my family. I miss you, and you are important to me. I want us to be the way we used to be."

To his surprise she answered, "Me too."

# Chapter 23

"Ashlynn, hurry up. We can't be late for the airport," Matthew hollered toward the back of the house.

Before rounding the kitchen door and swinging her backpack over one shoulder, Ashlynn hollered back, "I'm coming; I'm coming."

Adding his briefcase to other luggage beside the front door, Matthew turned to Brooke. "I really appreciate you going to work late this morning . . . helping us to get off. Thank you."

"No problem. Matt, hang on a moment, I need to check Ashlynn's bedroom and bath."

"Okay, we'll be loading the car. Please hurry," he said, but thought, geez . . . she called me Matt. She hasn't called me that in a long, long time.

After a few reminders and quick goodbyes, Matthew and Ashlynn were finally off to the airport. Although not her first airplane trip, Ashlynn looked uncomfortable as she followed behind her dad through the process of checking the luggage, getting their boarding passes, and arriving at the proper loading gate.

Once in their seats, Ashlynn watched the other passenger's get settled and started to tremble. Her eyes were glued to the flight attendant as she displayed the oxygen mask, discussed safety features of the airplane, and pointed out the various exits. As they waited to take-off, Ashlynn tapped her dad on the shoulder and said, "Dad, I'm scared. I try not to think about being up in the air, but I'm afraid."

"That's okay Sweetheart. I'm not too fond of flying either. I've lost count of the number of times I've taken-off and landed. I'm still not a fan of flying. I'll tell you what I do each and every time I fly. Maybe it will help you cope. First, we can hold hands." Smiling, "That's something I can't do when flying alone. Next, I breathe slowly in and out before saying a brief prayer. Lastly, I keep my eyes closed from the time we start down the runway until hearing the landing gear raised and locked.

"What if I can't hear it?" she questioned.

"Well, as soon as we're up, they'll make an announcement about something—like welcome aboard, serving drinks, or flight time to our destination. If all else fails, I remind myself of what a friend once told me. 'Doesn't do any good to worry. Can't do anything about it anyway. You might as well sit back and enjoy the flight . . . even look out the window.'"

"So Dad, do you like to look out the window cuz the shades down?" she quizzed but already knew the answer.

Grinning, he replied, "Nope, of course not."

Once they'd leveled off and had been welcomed aboard, Ashlynn asked, "What research am I helping with?"

"How did you know about that?" Matthew asked.

"Mom told me. Is it true?"

"It is. I'll give you some background while we fly . . . unless you'd rather read?"

"My books are in the overhead storage. I forgot to get one out before we sat down."

"It's no problem to get it if you want me to."

"No, it's okay. Tell me how I'm going to help."

"Really . . . talking instead of reading. Aren't you being wild and crazy," he said with a chuckle.

Stopping in front of the massive front entrance, Matthew asked, "Well, what do you think?"

Staring in obvious awe, Ashlynn stammered, "It's incredible.

"Wait till you see what's inside," he said with obvious anticipation for what was coming.

"Dad, did you choose the name because of the weeping willows?"

"Not me, but I'm sure—a long time ago—someone did. It was originally called Willowland Manor and was a cotton plantation. Now, it's Willowland Resort, because it's more than just the manor."

"So, manor means house . . . right? Is the house gone?" Ashlynn questioned.

"No, the manor's still here, but it's been remodeled for parties, weddings, and the like. It still has a few exclusive guest bedrooms for those who want to stay in an antebellum setting. That means before the Civil War."

"Dad, I know. I learned all that stuff in school."

"Sorry, a lot of people don't. I didn't until starting this project. Let me tell you what else I'm going to show you. There's a new hotel, golf course, clubhouse, and a paddleboat casino."

"Ooh, do I get to see the casino boat?"

"Not yet. It's being refurbished. It will be transported here before the Grand Opening." As if waiving his hand through the air—like reading a big sign—he added, "The launch of Atlantic City of the South."

"But I can see the rest . . . can't I?"

"Of course you can. That's why you're here . . . and to help me."

Placing the car in gear, he drove slowly up the entranceway road, pointing out different landscape additions they'd recently completed. As they approached the manor, Ashlynn's eyes opened wide with wonderment. "This is amazing. How did you make it look so old, yet seem so new?"

"Well, it hasn't been easy, and part of my latest problem . . . the one you're going to help me with."

"Huh," she responded, obviously confused. "I know nothing about old buildings."

"Since the building was part of the original plantation and very old, it is considered a historical landmark. That means certain regulations need to be precisely followed. For instance the outside can't be changed without permission—which by the way . . . never happens. So the outside architecture must remain the same. Naturally, some of it needed to be repaired but could only be restored to its initial appearance."

Still confused, Ashlynn inquired, "Like what?"

"The porches, railings, trim, shutters . . . using the same previous designs. That sometimes creates a problem, because components are made differently now. Replacing sections or entire areas can mean having them custom made . . . expensive and time consuming.

"What about the inside? Can it be changed?"

"Good question. It's been renovated many times before. Let's drive around, and then we'll return for a look see inside."

"Dad, thank you for bringing me. This is really neat, and I'm having a great time."

"I am too," he answered, patting her knee affectionately.

As they drove slowly through the area between the manor and new hotel, they needed to stop several times to wait on men moving equipment and supplies. Almost to the clubhouse, he honked at George. Receiving a wave, they watched him jog over to the car. Practically sticking his head inside the car window, he quickly remarked, "Looks like you brought a helper along this time."

"I did. Ashlynn, this is George. George, my daughter, Ashlynn."

"Hi little lady. Who would think an ole ugly guy like your dad would have such a beautiful daughter?"

"Ugly . . . huh. See if you get a bonus when we're finished," Matthew joked.

"Sorry Boss, but you know me—honesty is the best policy. Speaking of that, have you been in the parlor yet?"

"Not yet. I've been showing Ashlynn around. Showing her what we've been doing here. That's our next stop. Thought I'd let her pick out where she wants to stay."

"Have fun. I'll catch up with you later," George replied, pushing away from the car.

"Thanks. I'll call you after I check out your find."

Driving around the perimeter of the golf course and clubhouse—with lots of oohs and ahhs from Ashlynn—they arrived back in front of the manor.

"Let's go inside first. We'll come back a little later for the luggage . . . except I need to grab my briefcase real quick."

Matthew opened the manor's unlocked door and stepped back, waiting with anticipation for Ashlynn to enter first.

"Wow, this is so beautiful. Look at this wallpaper. Oh my gosh, I love it. Is this the way it looked way back when?"

"I hope so. That's what we were trying to achieve."

"Mom would really like this," Ashlynn commented. Already stepping away from the entryway and into the parlor, her father didn't quite hear what she'd said. He was anxious to see what George called him about at the office. George was absolutely right. What he saw was not only unbelievable but also a problem. On a table before him were the various items George removed from behind a fake wall in a room upstairs. Items undoubtedly hidden away for over a century. Glancing around at the very old memorabilia, he noticed a pair of plastic gloves—placed carefully by the edge of the table—and marveled at George's good sense to use them. The most interesting item to him—placed in the center—was the biggest Bible he'd ever seen with the name: Hattin embossed in gold lettering on the front. Unlike most of the other objects on display, it looked in perfect condition. He wanted to peek inside but after talking to corporate, he shouldn't for fear of causing damaging to it. After calling Ashlynn to come to where he was, he continued to look closely at the other objects, being careful not to touch any of them.

Thinking Ashlynn had taken a long time to join him, she finally walked into the parlor but didn't seem interested in what he pointed out. Looking at the objects for a minute or two, she asked, "Dad, can I stay in one of the bedrooms upstairs?"

"Sure, why not? How'd you know there were bedrooms upstairs?"

"Duh, I've already been up there."

"Which one did you pick?"

"The prettiest one . . . of course. Well, they're all pretty but this one looks out at the gigantic weeping willows."

"I think all of the rooms on that particular side look out at the willows," Matthew responded.

"True, but it's closest to the trees. I like it the best, and it has the prettiest wallpaper."

"Okay, let's get our stuff. You can show me which one."

Entering the room and placing her luggage next to the bed, Matthew commented with a grin, "Good choice. I'm going to see what room is close-by . . . and the second prettiest."

Gone a moment, he returned and said, "I'll be right across the hall if you need me. By the way staying with as much originality as possible, this room has no attached bathroom. Are you okay with that?"

"Yeah, it will be different . . . and fun. I mean there is a bathroom somewhere . . . right?"

"Come with me, and I'll show you. It's down at the end of the hall on the right side." When almost there, Matthew abruptly stopped. "I want to look inside this room." Opening the door and turning on the light, the small room was in total disarray.

Ashlynn remarked, "What happened? I thought you said the manor was all fixed except for a few minor details."

"Well, we thought it was. Remember the objects I showed you in the parlor?"

"The room next to the entryway?" she asked.

"Yes, that one." Then pointing, he added, "See the hole in the wall over there; this room is going to be used for upstairs storage. It has no window, so it was decided to put in a reverse vent but had a problem going into the room from the other side or from the roof. Long story short, they found those objects in an unknown space between the two rooms. Someone hid them away a long time ago. Imagine that, left there undisturbed for all these years."

"Dad, what will you do with them?"

"I'm talking to the Historical Society tomorrow. Hopefully, we can get some direction from them. The conglomerate didn't purchase personal possession not on the declaration list. I brought the list with me, so before I call and ask, maybe you can help me cross-check the list against the items downstairs. I doubt if any of them will match, but I need to know for sure."

"Should we do it now?"Ashlynn asked excitedly.

"Let's do it early tomorrow. Besides, I know how much you like to read, and you haven't had time today. We've kinda gotten off track. I still need to show you the bathroom . . . remember?"

Looking around the big bathroom and the enormous bathtub with weird claw feet, Ashlynn asked, "Dad, can I leave my stuff in here or will there be other people using it?"

"We'll be sharing it. No one else is staying here so leave whatever you like. I usually stay in a room in the new hotel, so I'll tell a housekeeper—hired in the interim to clean for special visitors from time to time—to come by daily to freshen up our rooms."

"I can do it. I'm not helpless like Mom thinks."

"I know Sweetie. It's just that this is vacation time for you . . . fun time. And Ashlynn, I don't think Mom thinks you're helpless."

"She always wants things to be in a certain place . . . just perfect like."

"I don't know about that. Well, she does get upset with me if I don't pick up after myself. Let's not worry about any of that. I want to spend as much time with you as I can before you go back to school. You can be my new personal assistant. Would you like that?"

Receiving a big smile and nod, Matthew determined she agreed.

Let's go back to our rooms and get settled in. Meet you in the hall shortly, and we'll find something interesting to eat. Sound like a winner?"

"Perfect . . . I'm hungry," she answered before skipping down the hall."

By the time they'd eaten and toured the area again, Ashlynn began to yawn. "Maybe we should head to bed early," Matthew remarked. "We've had a busy day after getting up early this morning."

"Whenever. Did you call Mom?" Ashlynn asked.

"Yes, and she seemed glad I called, glad we were here, and glad we are having a good time."

"I tried to call but got her message. I'll call her tomorrow," Ashlynn said before yawning again.

"So, tell the truth. Are you really having a good time? Not having withdrawals from not reading . . . are ya?"

"Dad . . . really? Why do you keep talking about me reading?"

"Every time I'm home; you are reading non-stop. Your mother says you spend ninety percent of your time with your face in a book."

"That's cuz you and Mom are always arguing. Mom's too busy to do anything with me or tells me I'm doing something the wrong way. It's easier to read. That way, she leaves me alone. Besides, all of my friends from school are on vacation, so there's nothing else to do."

"Mom and I will work on it. Don't get me wrong . . . reading is good, but being here with your dad at Willowland Resort in Mississippi is much better."

"I totally agree," Ashlynn replied.

# Chapter 24

Ashlynn woke suddenly from a deep sleep, thinking lightning had lit-up the room. Not unlike the beginning of a New Jersey storm, she listened for the accompanying thunder to follow with a boom, but all remained quiet. Sliding into her slippers, she rushed to the window to look out, expecting to see it raining. However, the sky was clear; the moon easily visible.

That's odd, she thought. Turning to go back to bed, she glanced below the window, seeing a young black woman in a white nightgown. She seemed to be motioning to her—more like beckoning for her to come out. Wondering why someone would be outside in the middle of the night, she tried to open the window but couldn't. When she looked down again, the person was gone. What should she do? Thinking it might be a worker's wife or girlfriend who needed help; her first thought was to wake her father. Continuing to watch the spot where she saw her, Ashlynn decided if she came back, she'd definitely get her dad. After a few minutes of watching as far as she could see in all directions, she concluded all was okay and went back to bed.

By early morning as she hurried to dress—not wanting to hinder her dad's daily routine—last night's incident was forgotten.

After finishing breakfast—consisting of a boxed meal heated in the microwave at the new but not completed hotel's kitchen—they drove around the complex, stopping numerous times for Matthew to receive progress updates.

Almost back to the front of the manor, Matthew remembered he'd forgotten to check-out the new wall surrounding the side parking lot. "I need to look at something. Do you want to go with me or stay and start checking the objects in the parlor?" he asked.

"I should start on my job," she answered with a lilt in her voice.

"That's what I like to hear. Such an eager beaver, you are."

When Matthew returned and entered the parlor, Ashlynn volunteered, "Nothing matched."

"I expected as much but needed to be sure. Thanks for helping with that. I'll call the Historical Society to see if this can be handled over the phone."

"Would it be okay if I look around outside?"

"Sure, but watch out for delivery trucks. Please don't wander far. It's a big area, and you could get lost."

"Dad, I'm not a little girl anymore. Oh, I forgot to tell you. A young black lady was below my window last night. I tried to open the window to ask if she needed help but couldn't. It was stuck."

"It's the new paint. It makes the windows stick, especially when not used. We'll go through and fix it on the final walk-through. Was the lady calling out for help?"

"No, just motioning for me to come down . . . I think."

"That's odd," he replied.

"I hope she's all right. When I couldn't get the window up and looked back, she was gone."

"That's interesting. She was probably a worker's friend who'd had one too many and looking for a ride. Don't worry about it. When we go out again, I'll ask George about it. He has a pretty good handle on what's happening around here. Ashlynn, let me know if you get bored. I'm afraid this is my life when I'm here on the property . . . in and out and driving around to check on job sights."

"I could never get bored here. There is something new to see or do every day. Besides, I like it here. I want to see everything before I go back. So, I'm off to explore. See ya later."

"Have fun but don't be gone too long."

"Okay," she hollered back, already down the front steps.

Watching Ashlynn leave, Matthew realized—even though he was constantly busy—he was also lonely. One way or the other— even if it meant finding another job—when this project was finished, he wouldn't be separated from his family for this long again. Picking up the two lists, he was impressed by Ashlynn's attention to detail. She had recorded each article, placing information to the side and notations about its condition. Studying the list, he wanted to familiarize himself with it before calling.

Introducing himself and stating the reason for his call, Matthew was directed to a lady who seemed knowledgeable about Willowland Manor. They spoke about the history of the plantation in general terms before she offered, "You know . . . we had a young woman stop here some years ago. Let me see . . . what was her name?  Oh yes, it was Samantha, but I can't recall her last name. She was doing a magazine article on Southern plantations turned into hotels.  Such a bright, young lady . . . she was.  I remember she was especially interested in Willowland Manor's founding family and their descendants.  If you can hold on a moment, I'll fetch the file."

Matthew hadn't shared what items were in his possession but did confess none of them were on the company's declaration list attached to the purchase contract.  While waiting, he was surprised she hadn't specifically inquired about them.

"I'm back with the file," she offered.  "At my age just finding an old file—this one's about five years old—is a significant happening in my life."

Not knowing if she was serious or kidding, Matthew refrained from commenting.  As he listened for her to continue, there was a definite pause and a rustling of papers—like she was looking through the file.

Finally speaking, she said, "Let me see . . . yes, there is a note here.  Samantha called later to say she'd located the only descendant she could find from an internet ancestry site.  Said his name was Boyd Nelson and he lives in the state of Arkansas.  I remember her saying she was disappointed at not being able to talk to him.  If I remember correctly, she wasn't even certain if he was still alive.  Wait . . . there's more here.  I don't remember any of this.  Perhaps it was added when I was away.  There's a copy of an old newspaper article.  Yes, it's from Samantha also.  Let's see . . . umm, a bed and breakfast, the Southern Comfort Inn, formally the Bennington Hotel, and originally the Willowland Manor had a terrible accident. A Vernon Nelson accidently fell down the stairs while staying there. A witness said, "Mr. Nelson mumbled right before becoming quiet . . . something about a white sheet chasing him. Sorry, I'm rambling. Are you still there? Do you want me to send this information to you?"

"Yes, I'm here . . . just listening," he answered but wanted to return to the point of his call, "So let me see if I understand how this works. I must do my best to locate this person and have him sign a release . . . correct."

"Well . . . sorta correct. He has the right to keep some or all of the items . . . if he wants them. He can let you have them to display, or he can donate them to us. You or your legal department will need to have his signature notarized according to his wishes and submit the papers to the State of Mississippi. Keep in mind as a descendant with valid proof, the items are his personal property and belong to him."

"So, if I understand correctly, we are stuck in limbo until we learn this guy's wishes. Since we are opening the resort in a few months, is it possible to keep the objects until we locate him?"

"I don't know why not. I'm surprised the items weren't on the list from the previous owners. I'm sorry . . . did you mention what you came across?"

"I have a list of them. Would you like me to read it to you?"

"Yes, of course. Mercy . . . a list. This is exciting."

"There's an incomplete small tea set with a teapot which has a broken handle, three cups, and 4 saucers. Two of the saucers have chips and one is cracked. There are miscellaneous wooden animals: a pig, a horse, a snake, and three chickens . . . maybe a dog or goat. We're not sure. There is a cornhusk doll with a porcelain head. The majority of it has deteriorated, but the head and some of the ribbons are intact."

"Those are obvious children's toys from that period," she interjected.

"There is a photograph of three young boys in confederate uniforms but no names, and a large family Bible with the word: Hattin on the front."

"Sorry to interrupt again but the founding family of the Willowland plantation was named Hattin."

"That makes sense because there's also an old photograph of a fairly empty cemetery with a large gravestone which has the name Hattin on it. The words below the name are difficult to read. The photo is blurry."

"Interesting," she commented. "I'm looking at a picture taken by Samantha of the cemetery, but the Hattin gravestone is surrounded by many gravesites. Matthew, do get back to us if you are able to locate Mr. Nelson . . . will you? In fact I'd appreciate you letting me know the outcome one way or the other. We would love to display those items. I'm selfishly hoping he'll have no use for them and will donate them to us. Articles that survive are such a big part of our history. Time is fleeting, but true history is forever. Thank you for doing the proper thing."

"You're welcome. I've written down your name. You have my name, our company name, and telephone number. If I don't contact you personally, the legal folks will. Thanks again for your help."

Hanging up the receiver, Matthew looked around the new hotel's sparse office, wondering if everything would come together as scheduled for the Grand Opening.  Getting close to the end but still lots to do, he thought.  Feeling relived, he now had a good feeling about this situation being somewhat resolved and no longer a distraction.  The good news for everyone concerned, it wouldn't affect the project's completion.  Being thoughtful, he knew hectic times were just around the corner, accepting the crunch-time as a normal part of finishing up a large project like this one.

Noticing Ashlynn wasn't back, he wondered if she'd returned to the manor.  Did he tell her he was going to the hotel to call?  He couldn't remember.  He needed to find George and talk about a place for the objects until Boyd Nelson could be found.  Hopefully, it would be soon.  After deciding on a safe spot to keep the objects, he'd give the legal department a head's up on searching for Mr. Nelson.

Seeing Ashlynn walking between the manor and new hotel, Matthew called out to her.  "Hello, young lady.  I've been looking for you.  Hop in the car and tell me what you've been doing."

Seated and placing on her seat belt, she said, "You'll never guess what I found."

"I'll guess you're right so tell me."

"You know the cemetery photo—the one with the stuff in the parlor—well, I found the actual graveyard.  It's bigger than I expected and has a bunch of graves in it."

"I know.  We had to be careful about preserving it properly.  It was a real mess when it was discovered.  It was a pain-staking operation with lots of hands-on labor required."

"I can't wait until Mom sees it," Ashlynn responded. "She loves old cemeteries. She's weird that way, but you already know about that. So Dad, did you find out anything when you called?"

"Yes, I think so. At least I have a better understanding of what needs to be done. It seems there's one living relative who needs to give permission about the found objects. Once he's contacted, he can take possession of them, give them to us to display, or donate them to the Mississippi Historical Society."

"What if you can't find him?"

"We need to show due diligence that we tried. If all else fails, we'll donate the items ourselves. That's what George meant when he remarked about honesty being the best policy. Some people might have stashed the articles away or destroyed them. George said it was up to me but destroying the Bible seemed sinful to him. I agreed but didn't want the hassle either. I think it's going to work out and be okay. Anyway, having you here to help has made it all worthwhile.

"Dad, I really haven't done anything," she countered.

"Well, I think you have, and I'm the boss. Let's find George, get something to eat, and then I'll call the legal department.

As the day came to an end, Ashlynn and her father sat across from each other in the parlor, talking about her conversation with George. Matthew apologized for forgetting to ask George about the mystery person below her room's window.

"What's on the agenda for tomorrow," Ashlynn asked.

Grinning, he answered, "You sound just like your mother."

"I know. I say it a lot. Sometimes, I try to beat her before she says it to me."

"Tomorrow will be more of the same. Is there something you want to see or do?"

"George said they're having a cook-out tomorrow and many of the workers' family members are coming to celebrate the completion of the clubhouse. Are we going?"

"Darn it, I forgot to tell you. Sorry, guess I was concentrating on other things. I think it will be fun. We've been doing this monthly since the project started. It helps for everyone to interact and have a good time together away from work."

"How come Mom and I weren't invited?"

"I mentioned it to your mom many times, but she was never interested."

"I called Mom today," Ashlynn said.

"How did that go? Wait, I take that back. You don't need to tell me what you talked about, but did she happen to ask about me?"

"She said she was lonely. And . . . she said after the Grand Opening, she hoped we could be a real family again . . . together and all."

"Really, she said that?"

"Not exactly in those words . . . but close," she replied.

"Dad, did I tell you the person I saw from the window looked like she was wearing a night gown?"

"No, you didn't mention what she was wearing." After an uncomfortable pause, he added, "That's strange and makes no sense at all. I'll talk to George . . . for sure."

After another uncomfortable quiet moment, Matthew remarked, "With the table removed, this room looks a lot larger . . . don't you think?" Seeing Ashlynn nod in the affirmative, he continued, "I've got a surprise for you. It was delivered earlier today. Let's go into the big room and test it out."

Entering the banquet room, Matthew asked, "Do you see anything different?"

"Oh my gosh, it's beautiful. Can I play it?"

"Yes, or you can listen to it play."

"Really? I can't believe a grand piano is also a player piano."

Ashlynn sat down and started playing chopsticks. "Hey, is that what years of paying for piano lessons gets me?" Matthew asked.

Not answering, she began to play *The Old Rugged Cross.* When finished, there were tears in her father's eyes. "Mom said it was your favorite hymn, so I learned to play it without sheet music. I didn't mean to make you sad."

"It was also my mother's favorite hymn. Every time I hear it; I'm reminded of her and her funeral."

"You never talk about your parents. How come?" Ashlynn asked.

"That's a discussion for another time. How about on our trip home?"

"Okay, sounds like a plan but don't forget. Could you show me how to work the player part?" she asked with visible enthusiasm.

"Haven't a clue. That seems like a job for my personal assistant to handle," Matthew replied.

"I saw a box underneath it. Maybe the rolls or floppy discs are in there. We had an upright player piano in the Music Room at school, but I never gave it much attention." Smiling, she continued, "It was used to show us how something was supposed to sound. I remember when the roller part broke, they replaced it with one using floppies."

"Help yourself. Like I said; I have no idea. I'll see if it's plugged in. I can handle the plug part."

After some trial and error guessing, they listened to a classical piece which neither of them recognized. When Ashlynn began to yawn, Matthew commented, "I think it's time for bed. Do you want me to tuck you in like old times?"

"Only if you'll read me a bedtime story?" she answered and laughed.

"Don't push your luck unless you want to hear "Goldilocks and the Three Bears" from memory. That might be a tad too young for you but does bring back lots of memories."

"You think. Goodnight Dad."

"Goodnight Ashie."

# Chapter 25

Ashlynn woke to the sound of a rooster crowing. As she tried to put on her slippers, neither fit right. They felt tight and rough inside. Looking down, she understood why. Both feet were covered with dried mud. Her first reaction was . . . what in the world happened? Then wondered how mud could get on her feet without her knowledge? Looking back at the bed, dried dirt—obviously once mud—was smeared into the bed sheets and stood out against the white linens. Still not able to figure out the mud, she headed for the bathroom to wash her feet. As she hurried down the hall, she passed little balls of dried mud on the rug, seeing more on the stairs leading downward. Beginning to cry, she suddenly remembered going outside last night and why. Dad was gonna be really mad at her. What explanation could she give him that would justify what she'd done? For sure he wouldn't understand, and now she wasn't certain she did either. Even though it made perfect sense last night, now it didn't. What would the housekeeper think? Would she be forced to leave? If she could clean it up before anyone knew, especially her dad, could she keep her middle of the night outing a secret?

Hastily cleaning her feet in the bathtub and rinsing any remnants of dirt from the tub, she wet a rag to wipe off the smeared places on the sheets. Returning to her room, she quickly made the bed and hid her slippers before rushing out to find a dust pan and broom. Uh oh, too late. Meeting her father coming up the stairs, he smiled and said, "Good morning, Ashlynn." So far, so good, she thought. Relieved he'd not noticed the little clumps of dirt scattered about, she replied, "Hi Dad."

"Glad you're up and dressed. Why did you go out last night?" he asked with a serious expression. Not giving her time to answer, he followed quickly with, "Not a good idea. I hope you at least took a flashlight."

"No, I didn't need one. The moon was out and really bright." Losing her composure, she began to cry. "I tried to clean it up before you noticed. I'm sorry."

"Don't worry about the dirt. I'm more concerned about you. Ashlynn, you shouldn't go out by yourself at night . . . at least without letting me know what's happening. If you had a reason, you should have gotten me up. Trying to relieve the tension, he added, "Your trail of dried mud through the entryway, up the stairs, and to your room wasn't hard to miss . . . like Hansel and Gretel."

Still sobbing, she said, "I'm really sorry. The truth is . . . I didn't realize my feet collected mud. I thought they were just wet and cold. All I could think about was getting back into bed to get warm. Are you going to make me go home?"

"Honey, I'm not angry . . . just worried."

"Dad, if you'll show me where the broom is, I'll clean up the mess."

"No worries. I'll have it vacuumed. Let's go have something to eat."

"Dad, please don't be mad at me."

"Ashlynn, listen to me. I'm not mad . . . honest. Let's forget it ever happened."

"What if there's something's wrong with me? Maybe Mom was right to make me go to a therapist. Last night seemed like a good idea at the time. Now, it doesn't."

"Maybe you were sleepwalking. Have you done that before?" he asked.

"Not that I can remember. Does a person know what they're doing when they sleepwalk? Is it like a dream, but you're not really asleep? Maybe I've done this before, but Mom didn't tell me. If I wasn't sleepwalking, then there must be something wrong with me."

"Honey, calm down. I'll call your mom and see what she says."

"Will you tell me . . . even if it's bad?" Ashlynn asked pathetically.

"Yes, but no matter what, we both love you very much and will always want the best for you. Quit worrying. We'll get to the bottom of this."

As he followed closely behind Ashlynn into the hotel for breakfast, Matthew felt apprehensive . . . even afraid. If she was sleepwalking, he needed to figure out how to keep her safe from this happening again. The possibilities of what could happen were scary. He wished the security cameras were working. If Brooke was aware of this and didn't warn him, he'd be upset beyond words.

Driving toward the golf course, Ashlynn asked, "Dad, if I tell you something, do you promise not to make fun of me?"

"I promise, but why would you even consider I'd make fun of you?"

"You didn't ask why I went outside last night. How come?"

"I was concerned about you . . . more than why," he replied honestly.

"I saw the same black woman again during the night. She was in my room by the door and wanted me to come with her. It was sorta like a strange dream, yet it wasn't. She wasn't talking but using hand signals. I'm not sure how, but she let me know it was important for me to follow her. By the time I got out of bed, she was in the hall. When I was out in the hall, she was already at the bottom of the stairs. When I was almost to the bottom of the stairs, she was already outside. I remember thinking she must be in really good shape, because she moved so quickly. Before I knew it, I had followed her into the willow trees. I didn't have my slippers on and began to feel cold—like a cold breeze was sweeping around me—and my feet were wet. I gave up trying to catch up to her, so we could talk. I had this compelling feeling she wanted to tell me something important in private; otherwise why did she want me outside of the manor? Thinking she was in trouble, I told her to stop, because I was cold and going back. Then, she just disappeared. I couldn't see her anymore. I guess she hid behind a tree. I don't know; maybe I hurt her feelings, cuz I was leaving. Maybe I'm crazy? When I'm talking about what happened last night, it sounds really weird. Dad, please believe me. It isn't my imagination, and I'm not making this up."

"Is there a possibility you were dreaming, and in your dream you imagined what you should have done the previous time you saw her? Maybe you felt guilty about not asking if she needed help. Your mind can play silly tricks on you. I know mine does from time to time." As he tried to relieve her anxiety, he was more worried than ever.

"What about the mud? Why didn't I see it," she asked, staring directly into his face.

"You were cold and hurrying to get back. Just in case you were sleepwalking, we need to decide what to do. We certainly don't want this to happen again. Could you look up sleepwalking on the internet? The phone we bought you for Christmas should connect to the internet from here . . . I think. Did you bring it?"

Before she could answer, they arrived at the clubhouse parking area. "Ashlynn, please don't get out yet," Matthew said. He looked directly into her eyes and said, "I love you."

"I know. I love you too Dad, but . . . I don't want to cause you any trouble."

"Never," he answered.

# Chapter 26

"Good news," were the first words Matthew heard when he answered his cell phone. Listening intently to the head office attorney, he interrupted as little as possible and then only to clarify a misunderstood statement.

"So he'll be here tomorrow . . . that soon," Matthew remarked, wanting to make sure he heard what day correctly.

"Yes, he insisted on seeing the property in person before signing anything. I tried to set up a formal meeting, but—just between you and me and only my opinion—I think he wasn't tracking well."

"Meaning?" Matthew asked.

"He was slurring his words and repeated everything I said."

"When property was discussed, was he referring to the items or the land?" Matthew asked.

"Honesty, I'm not sure. He mentioned—more than once—how he wanted to claim what was rightfully his. Either way, I'm having the paperwork curried to you as we speak. It should arrive mid-morning tomorrow. The currier is also a notary and will remain there until this is settled. The papers are straight-forward but call if there's a problem."

"Thanks for your help," Matthew offered.

"Good luck. Let me know if I can be of further assistance."

Hanging up the receiver, Matthew looked for Ashlynn. Entering the clubhouse lobby, she was sitting with George. "Can I interrupt," he asked.

"Ashlynn and I were talking about tonight's cook-out. She's bringing pheasant under glass," George stated before chuckling.

"Not true, but I would if I could. Guess I better find out what pheasant in a glass is," she said with a shy shrug.

"It's a fancy dish. A whole pheasant served under a glass dome. I've never had the pleasure. How about you George?" Matthew asked.

"Not me either," George responded. Looking directly at Ashlynn, he said, "Don't worry about bringing anything to the cook-out little lady; we've got it covered." Then quickly added, "All you need to do is show up and have a good time."

"George, we need to talk," Matthew said seriously.

"Sorry Boss, what's up?"

"We've got a visitor coming tomorrow to look at the discovered memorabilia."

"That was fast. Is he the real deal?"

"Our attorney seems to think so. He sounds like a piece of work to me, but I'm keeping an open mind."

"What does that mean?" George asked.

Glancing at Ashlynn, Matthew said, "Ashlynn, George and I are going out front to look at the tables for tonight. I'll be back in a few minutes."

Once alone, Matthew repeated the information from the company's attorney. "It seems the last Hattin descendant has recently been released from a half-way house. Sounds like he's a low-life petty criminal who's been incarcerated for theft, drugs, and numerous run-ins with the law. Even arrested for two rapes but not convicted because the victims wouldn't testify against him. The attorney inferred he was under the influence when they talked. Not sure if he meant drugs or alcohol. I'll be glad when this is finally over. I wasn't hired to be a keeper of artifacts or a nursemaid to some unsavory person. I'm a project manager trying to get a job done for God's sake."

Keenly aware of his boss's displeasure and frustration, George offered, "I'll be here tomorrow and available if you need my help, but let's forget about him for now. Tonight should be about showing Ashlynn a good time and acknowledging the clubhouse personnel. I bet Ashlynn is tired of being around us old guys and not having fun with her own age group. The workers will be bringing their families and some are teenagers about her age. Your daughter was really worried about not bringing a dish tonight . . . saying it was poor manners to arrive empty-handed. You're doing a good job at parenting."

"Can't take any credit there. That's all her mother's doings. I haven't been around much in the parenting department, but that's changing after the Grand Opening. On a personal note thank you George for your kindness to Ashlynn and for your leadership with the clubhouse personnel. It turned out better than I envisioned. You've done a terrific job."

Returning inside, Matthew saw Ashlynn huddled in a corner chair, feverishly pushing her fingers against her phone. She didn't look up when he approached.

"Hi, whatcha doing?" he asked, purposely wanting to engage her about cook-out plans.

Continuing to move her fingers, she answered, "Looking up sleepwalking."

"And?" he questioned with raised eyebrows . . . unnoticed by Ashlynn.

Looking around to make sure they were alone before answering, "I'm not sure. Some of it makes sense, but some doesn't."

"Did you hear me tell George that Boyd Nelson is coming tomorrow?" Matthew asked.

"Not exactly. I didn't hear his name . . . only that a visitor was coming. You obviously didn't want me to hear more. Dad, I might be a headcase, but I'm not dumb."

"Ashlynn, don't make remarks like that. You are neither one. This guy doesn't sound like a nice person, so while he's here; I want you be scarce . . . okay?"

"Okay. Is George still outside?"

"Not sure . . . why?"

"I want to ask him something."

"Try to catch him," he answered but wondered what she could possibly ask George that she couldn't ask him. Hearing her call out to George and still curious, he walked to the window to look out. They talked for a minute or so before Ashlynn rushed back inside.

"Dad, can I go with George to look at something?"

"Yes, but what are you up to?"

"I heard a rooster crow this morning, and George is taking me to see the chickens on the back side of the golf course. It's okay if I go see them . . . right?"

"Of course . . . have fun. See you when you get back. I'll be either at the hotel or in the manor . . . probably in the manor."

Thinking ahead and doing his best to maintain his composure and not worry, Matthew methodically gathered a few items for Ashlynn's safety. While waiting patiently for Ashlynn to return from her outing with George, he had a lot to think about. Brook was joining them tomorrow to surprise Ashlynn, and now he had to deal with Boyd Nelson coming too. He started to suggest the possibility of putting off the guy for a few days, but it didn't seem appropriate to ask due to personal reasons. Not pleased and since he had no choice in the matter, he'd somehow handle it.

Almost an hour later, Ashlynn walked into the manor and found her father waiting in the parlor. Next to him on the sofa were two big flashlights, a string of bells, and something which resembled a hastily put-together wind chime.

Pointing beside him, Ashlynn questioned, "What's all that?"

Expecting the inquiry, Matthew was prepared with his answer. "Protection," he quickly replied.

"Protection from what?" she queried.

"From you escaping and causing me more worries."

"Dad, are you still mad at me?" she asked before dropping her head.

"No, definitely not, but your dad can worry . . . can't he? Isn't that my main job?"

Without commenting and changing the subject, she said . . . almost bubbling, "Oh, guess what? I got to see the chickens. They're amazing. The workers built them a little place to nest, and George told me they lay eggs every day. They eat omelets, egg salad sandwiches, and snack on hard boiled eggs. Isn't that some-thing? Dad, there are real honest to goodness chickens."

"How about that. I had no idea. This is definitely a different way of life from where we live." His turn to change the subject, he continued, "We should leave in about an hour. I need to touch bases with George on the bonuses before the clubhouse workers start arriving."

"Can I do anything to help?" Ashlynn asked.

"You can take the flashlights to your room and place the other stuff on the floor outside your door."

"Are you serious?" she asked, her hands placed squarely on her hips.

"Dead serious. I want to hear if you leave your room. When we come back from the cook-out, and you go to bed; I'm placing the stuff on your door handle."

"Whatever," she answered with obvious disapproval.

Stopping in mid-stride, she turned back and said, "Dad, shouldn't we take something to the cook-out?"

"Oh yeah, I forgot to talk to you about that. I've always taken care of the plates, napkins, and utensils for the cook-outs. A large sup-ply has accumulated in storage through the months, so we're good. Tonight, I'll be passing out bonus checks to the workers who finished the clubhouse before the scheduled completion date. This will be the last time some of them will be working here. It's both a celebration and a time to say goodbye. They'll be moving on to other jobs."

"That's sad," Ashlynn remarked.

"Yes and no. That's how construction work goes. They know when a job starts, it will eventually end." Smiling, he continued,

"The Grand Opening is not far off, and I can hardly wait for Willowland Resort to officially open."

"Cuz that means you'll come home for good. Will you miss this place?"

"I'll miss the acquaintances I've made . . . people like George, but being home with you and your mom full time will be dream come true and long overdue."

"I'm off to change and get ready for the party," Ashlynn replied.

Matthew marveled at how Ashlynn appeared more outgoing and self-sufficient in only a few days' time. Grinning, he watched her navigate the stairs, clinking and clanking with each upward step.

# Chapter 27

*I*t had been six months since Boyd Nelson's release from Elayn Hunt Correctional Prison at St. Gabriel, Louisiana. Part of the terms for his early release was a four month mandatory stay in a New Orleans Mid-City District half-way house. Having stayed there for the minimum allotted time—practically still a prisoner—he'd been outed on the anticipated move-out date for failure to comply with their sober living rules. While waiting for his delayed trip money—promised to fund his transportation home—he received a phone call from a New Jersey lawyer. Ready to tell him to take a hike—thinking he was speaking to the wrong person—Boyd soon realized the guy was for real. Setting aside any notions of whether or not he was actually the person the lawyer was looking for; all he could see were dollar signs floating by in front of his eyes. Besides, since he had no home to go to, accepting the transportation money was just a rouse anyway and never a true option for its use. More than likely, he would have immediately used the money to purchase a weapon and drugs. After the phone call, he had new plans for the money.

Asking to stay a few more days at the half-way house, his request was promptly denied and openly given no consideration by those holier-than-thou jerks running the place. Pocketing the trip money, he used some of it to crash in a cheap bug-infested room, staying on a day-to-day basis until he found Snake, Big Bud, or both.

He walked briskly across Jackson Square, hearing some dude hawking "Hey Baby, Nawleens is where it's happenin'. Look what I got for you." Well, it wasn't happenin' for him at the moment, but it would soon, especially after he had a drink . . . lots of drinks would be even better. He knew exactly where he was going, zigzagging through street musicians, mimes, and tricksters until making a beeline to Jake's Place on Bourbon Street. While searching for his bros, Jake's would be his first stop. Once found, he would drink to oblivion on their tab. They owed him big time for taking the full rap for the robbery and not ratting them out.

Entering Jake's and going straight to the bar, he stood there for a moment before calling out to the bartender—who was clearly playing grab-ass with a cute blonde at the end of the bar—"Hey barkeep, a little service over here." Pitching down a ten spot, he waited—but not patiently—to be acknowledged.

"Yeah, what can I get you," the bartender asked, obviously perturbed for being summoned away from his lady friend.

Asking for a shot of whiskey, he rhythmically thumped his fingers against the bar's slick polished wood. Once served, he watched the bartender hurry back to the giggling blonde. Quickly downing the shot, he peered around, noticing only one other person sitting on a bar stool at the opposite end of the bar. Being ignored, he stated sarcastically, "Hate to bother you again but give me another shot. That is . . . if it's not too much trouble, and you're not too busy." Then added loudly, "Make it quick . . . would ya? I'm in a hurry."

"Be right with you," the bartender answered in an unruffled manner.

Downing his shot, he asked, "You seen Big Bud or Snake around?"

"Who's asking," the bartender quizzed.

"Boyd."

"Boyd who?" the bartender inquired.

"Just Boyd," he replied, waiting for an answer.

"Haven't seen them lately. You might find them at Chester's on Decatur Street."

"I'll settle up," Boyd stated, pushing the ten dollar bill forward.

After collecting payment—the exact amount to cover the two shots—the bartender remarked, "Later."

"What . . . no change?" Boyd asked.

"No, that covers it," was answered along with a direct stare.

Turning away, Boyd mumbled loud enough to be heard, "Damn rip-off."

The customer's comment easily heard, the bartender remarked sarcastically but with a smile, "Thanks for coming in. See you again big spender."

Walking easily to Chester's Bar—the name flashing in neon lights was a dead giveaway—Boyd didn't remember it being there before his incarceration. Once inside, he took a moment to adjust to the dimly lit room. Placing another ten dollar bill on the bar, he asked for a shot of house whiskey. As he looked around, he was the only patron there but heard pool balls hitting together in a connecting room.

Before the bartender set up the shot, Boyd interrupted him by saying, "Wait a minute; change it to a double." As the whiskey was placed in front of him, Boyd commented, "I'm looking for a couple of buddies of mine and hear they come here from time to time."

"I might or might not know who you're looking for. How about a name?"

"Snake or Big Bud. I've lost touch with them. Been gone for awhile."

"And your name?" questioned with a suspicious frown and head tilt.

"Boyd . . . just Boyd." Waiting for an answer, Boyd finally remarked, "Either you do or don't know them. It's a simple question so quit with the third degree."

Without replying the bartender left and exited through a door next to the bar. After a couple of minutes, he returned and said, "Follow me, there's someone on the phone for you."

Taking the phone off the small cluttered desk, Boyd asked, "Yeah, who's this?" Listening, he answered back, "Yes, it's me, and I'm out. No, I'm not looking to party . . . maybe later. Right now, I need transportation . . . a car, truck, or something to get me to Mississippi. Yes, dummy, I'm at Chester's. Get your ass down here pronto." Hearing several excuses, Boyd finally interrupted, "Not my problem. You owe me . . . one hour."

While waiting and even though already feeling the warmth of the booze settling in, he ordered another shot and thought about his intended plans. Let's see . . . he was supposed to be at Willowland Resort in two more days, but he was going to show up tomorrow. He wanted to get the lay of the land before seeing what deal he could make with them. They'd obviously gone to a lot of trouble to find him and big companies don't do that out of the goodness of their hearts, he reasoned.

When Snake walked in, he first nodded to the bartender before looking around the room. Spotting Boyd, he followed his pointing finger to a secluded corner booth across the room. Once seated opposite each other, Snake said, "Hey Man, what's cookin'?"

"No . . . how the hell are ya? No . . . it's been a long time since we've talked. No . . . thanks for sitting your ass in a cell for me for three years. Where's Big Bud?"

"He took off a year ago. The heat's been on. It's getting harder and harder to move shit, so he left to find his old lady and kid."

"Well, get ready for the big time. I'm about to collect on my inheritance."

"What you talkin' about. You ain't got no family," Snake answered with confusion on his face.

"I'm talking big bucks, but I gots to get to Mississippi to claim it," he replied excitedly.

"How much you got for a car?" Snake asked, seemingly more interested.

"Get real. I ain't got crap right now. That's where you come in. You gotta beg, borrow, or steal me a car . . . by tomorrow. You understand what I'm saying."

"I don't know Bro. I'll try."

"No, you'll do better than try. You'll do it. If not, you know what I'm capable of doing. Don't run either, cuz I'll find you. I'll see you tomorrow with wheels and bring me a phone."

"Man, this is real short notice."

"Not my problem. I'm not askin'; I'm tellin'." Pointing toward the door, he added, "Get movin'. Time's a-wastin'."

As he watched Snake leave, he could feel the alcohol doing its job. The feeling of warmth was traveling up and down his body. He thought about hooking-up with a gutter whore, but decided it wasn't a good idea to get sidetracked. Since he'd waited this long to get laid, he could wait a little longer. Soon, he'd have enough cash to find a pro to service him properly.

After trading Snake's phone and his remaining money for speed—enough to keep him going through his Willowland adventure—Boyd was finally traveling north in Snake's piece of junk car. With each mile of his excursion he could feel the crystal kicking in; his body tingling with activity. He was definitely smarter and more cleaver than any corporate dude they could throw his way. Full of himself, he felt on top of the world, viral, and in total control.

*Chapter 28*

The cook-out drawing to a close, Matthew walked to the front of the table area to make an announcement: "I would like to thank everyone involved in creating this spectacular resort and especially those associated with the building and completion of this beautiful clubhouse behind us. When I first started working here, the clubhouse was my special project. I passed it on to George. Thank you George for a terrific job . . . well done. Would the clubhouse workers please step up front and join me."

As the men walked forward, cheers, whistles, and applause followed them. Once the group gathered beside Matthew, he continued, "The company has a gift for each of you in appreciation for an outstanding job. I personally thank you, and the company thanks you for completing the clubhouse thirty days early . . . an unbelievable accomplishment."

Handing out the last of the bonus checks—each equal to one month's pay—the wind suddenly came up. Lightening was noticeable in the distance, so Matthew made another announcement: "Folks, it looks like a storm is coming our way. Sorry to put a damper on the party, but we better clean-up before the wind blows everything away. Thank you all for coming."

Looking for Ashlynn, he saw her talking and laughing with a group of teenagers. Watching for a moment, it was clearly apparent she was having a good time. He hated to tell her it was time to leave. Approaching her, his cell phone went off. Glancing at the screen, it was Brooke.

Answering, "Hi, please don't tell me you're cancelling tomorrow's trip."

"No, I'm here. Well, maybe forty-five minutes away."

"Are you serious? That's wonderful, but what changed your mind?" he asked with enthusiasm and puzzlement.

"There's a storm coming in from the gulf. If I waited until tomorrow, I probably couldn't get out. As it was, I took the last available plane today. I didn't want to ruin Ashlynn's surprise."

"That's great. She has no idea you're coming. She'll be just as surprised tonight as tomorrow. We're about to finish up the cook-out. I can see lightning off in your direction, and the wind is already here. Keep me informed on your progress. We're trying to clean-up and get inside before it starts raining."

"It's already started where I am. Not raining hard . . . just sprinkling. I hate to drive in the rain so wish me luck. I don't know how to turn on the rental car's windshield wipers. If it rains any harder, I'll pull over and figure it out, she answered and groaned."

"Be careful. I'll see you in about an hour. Brooke, I love you."

"Love you too, Bye."

Waving at Ashlynn to get her attention, Matthew watched her say something to the boy she was chatting with before walking toward him. Stopping in mid-stride—as if forgetting something— she turned and waved back before saying, "See you tomorrow."

"What's that all about," Matthew asked.

"He's been taking piano lessons since he was seven years old, and he's the same age as me. He's totally fascinated by the grand piano being a player piano. I told him to come by tomorrow, and I'd show it to him."

Without commenting and thinking about Brooke being with them, he commented, "I think it's time to call it a night. Have you had a fun time?" he asked but already knew the answer by her demeanor.

"Yes, lots. The kids I met are really cool. They didn't know I lived in New Jersey but knew I was from up north. They told me I was pretty nice for a Yankee."

"What did you say to back to them?" he asked with a grin.

"I said they were pretty nice for Southerners."

"Good answer. Let's head for the manor. Rain is coming."

As Matthew parked the car, the rain had progressed from a few sprinkles to a downpour. Rushing inside but not quickly enough to keep from getting drenched, Ashlynn said, "Thanks Dad. I really had a blast tonight." After a big sneeze, she added, "The boy I told you about really made me laugh. He also said for a Yankee, I was all right."

"I'm glad it was a fun time for you. That was my main concern . . . and your mom's. It's been great to have you here with me. What are your plans for tonight?" he asked casually. "Going to bed early, reading one of your books, or playing the piano?"

"That's a good idea," she answered

"Which one?" he asked.

I think I'll go through the box to see if I can find a song I recognize. What are you going to do?"

"I need to get my ducks in order for the meeting tomorrow with Mr. Nelson. Hearing the rain blowing firmly against the window panes, he commented, "Boy, it's really raining now. Did you happen to bring along any rain gear?"

"No, guess I should have," she answered before coughing.

"Uh oh, maybe you should get those wet clothes off and into something dry."

"Would it be okay if I put on my nightgown and came downstairs in it?"

"Of course you can. I've got a housecoat hanging on the back of the door in my room . . . if you need it."

"Thanks, I am a little cold. Is it the same old black one you've worn forever?" Without answering, he started to get up but she quickly added, "I'll get it."

While Ashlynn was upstairs changing, Matthew's phone rang. It was Brooke again. "Hi . . . almost here?" he asked with surprise.

"Matt, I need your help. I don't know what to do," replied with noticeable anxiety in her voice.

"Calm down. What's the matter?"

"I pulled off the road to find the windshield wipers and got stuck. I tried to get the car back on the road but couldn't. What should I do?" she asked again and started to cry.

"Can you tell me where you are? Describe something around you?"

"The navigation system says I'm twenty-five miles to my destination. I can't see any landmarks . . . just trees on both sides of the road. I don't remember passing anything notable either. Guess I was watching straight ahead and being careful cuz of the rain."

"I think it will be faster if I come to you rather than call for a tow truck. Make sure the emergency flashers are on. What color is the car?"

"It's gray, and I did find the flasher button. My feet are all muddy, and I'm sopping wet."

"Honey, I'll be there as soon as I can. Should I tell Ashlynn what's happening or bring her along. What do you think?"

"No, I still want to surprise her. Will she be all right until we get back? I've lost track of the time. It's dark out, so is it late?" she asked with concern but no longer crying. "If she's asleep, I don't want to take the chance of her sleepwalking . . . especially in the rain.

"No, she's changing for bed. Said she was cold, and I've heard her coughing. Probably better she doesn't go out in the rain. We both got a tad wet earlier. I'll be there as quickly as I can. I'll hurry."

Disconnecting the call, he hollered upstairs to Ashlynn, "Have you finished changing?" Not receiving a response and wanting to hustle, he started up the stairs to look for her. Stepping over the noise makers, he stuck his head in her room. Not there and assuming she was in the bathroom, he walked in that direction. Halfway down the hall, she came out and sneezed.

"Bless you. Are you okay," he asked.

"Yeah, I think I'm catching a cold . . . no big deal."

"I've got a quick errand to run. Should be back in an hour . . . hour and a half tops. Are you gonna be okay while I'm gone?"

"Dad . . . really? There you go again. I'll be fine. I'm not a little kid anymore. I'm almost seventeen."

"I know. I just want to make sure you're comfortable with being here by yourself for a little while."

"I'll be fine," she answered before sneezing twice, followed by a cough.

"There's aspirin in my travel case in the bathroom." Receiving no comment, he said, "Okay, I'm off. I've got my phone with me."

"Dad, if you're not back before I go to bed, I promise to put your noise makers on the outside of the door before I close it. Please don't worry about me."

"Good girl but I'm sure I'll be home before then. Have fun with the piano. By the way—as a Southerner would say—you look mighty fetching in my housecoat."

"Yeah . . . right. If your definition of too big and too long is fetching, but it sure is warm and comfy."

Smiling, he blew her a kiss and was out the front door.

# Chapter 29

Entering the Willowland Resort's main gate, Boyd followed the road until encountering two buildings. Turning at the arrowed Clubhouse sign, he continued down the road to see what else was on the property. Marveling at the surroundings, he came upon a dozen or so parked cars lining both sides of the road, leaving barely enough room to pass between them. Curious to see what was going on, he parked further down the road and carefully made his way toward a group of people. Most of them were sitting at tables in front of a fancy building; a few standing nearby and talking. Surprised, he'd not expected to see this many people around a worksite in the early evening hours. While considering how to blend in, his eyes caught sight of a cute girl laughing and talking to a boy leaning against a tree. She reminded him of his ex-wife, Pearl. Slightly younger but constantly placing her hair behind her ears, she had the same flirty attitude and movements as Pearl. Boy, would he like to have some of that, he thought.

Hiding behind a tree, he thought about what to do next, deciding to go back to the car and continue his look see of the entire property. If the rest was anything like he'd already seen, it was mighty impressive. At one time this all belonged to his ancestors.

How about that! For whatever reason they wanted to find him—
and they weren't fooling him one little bit—it had to be for more
than a few trinkets from the past. And for whatever reason—one
way or the other—he was going to capitalize on his good fortune.

Opening the car door, a bitter cold wind smacked him in the
face. That seemed odd for summertime, he thought. Sitting in the
car to determine which way to go, the sky darkened and lightening
appeared in the distance. Driving slowly around the perimeter of
the golf course, he knew it wouldn't be long before it started to rain.
Damn it, he'd not thought to bring along a rain jacket when gathering stuff. His mind kept jumping from one thought to another,
remembering the main priority of driving around the property was
to look for another exit . . . just in case he needed to go to plan B
and make a hurried escape. Important to find out what was available—one way or the other—he was leaving with valuables.

Having slowly encompassed the golf course, Boyd found himself back where he started but behind a car with a recognized passenger . . . the pretty girl he'd noticed earlier. Now almost dark,
he was curious to see where they were going, expecting them to
at least follow the road which led out of the resort. However,
approaching the entranceway road, the driver veered off and drove
to the side of the big house. Why would a worker stop there?
Continuing to wonder, he assumed it could be an older worker and
his daughter stopping to pick something up or maybe an older guy
with his young foxy girlfriend sneaking away. Puzzled, when he
talked to the attorney and insisted on staying at the new resort, he
was told no one occupied the premises yet. As he watched where

the guy parked, he didn't want to risk being noticed so would find somewhere else to park when he came back.

Continuing on, Boyd drove down the entranceway and exited the property. About a mile down the main road he found a safe place to pull off and wait. It wasn't long before a caravan of cars passed by. Waiting several minutes more for additional stragglers to pass, he assumed the cars were coming from the clubhouse gathering; the people leaving to get out of the rain. Searching through the pile on the passenger seat, he felt confident he'd brought along the necessary items to explore the three buildings . . . except something to keep him dry until getting inside of them.

The rain turning into a downpour, either he needed to find shelter or stay in the car for the night. Grinning, one of those fancy buildings would surely be available. After all, they were all supposed to be unoccupied. If unfinished and not available for the paying public; he reckoned a Willowland descendant could lay claim to a dry spot for one night. The lawyer made it clear the resort wouldn't be open until the Grand Opening but didn't say exactly when it would be.

After a lengthy lull in traffic, he started the car, turned on the headlights, and then the windshield wipers. Great, only one side moved, but luckily for him the driver's side worked. As he prepared to pull out onto the main road, he waited for a single car to pass. How about that—the same guy and car—but this time alone. Interesting . . . the pretty young gal must have been left behind. But for how long, he wondered, as other possibilities popped into his mind.

Driving down the entranceway road again, he couldn't help but wonder if this was the same road his ancestors used when traveling to and from the plantation house. Deciding to park on the opposite side from where the man parked earlier, he found a secluded blacktopped area. It was between the two buildings and seemingly convenient for leaving in either direction. Placing a dark ski mask over his face and grabbing a flashlight, he jumped out into the rain. Damn, it was a cold rain too. Again thinking . . . a cold rain in summer seemed strange.

Approaching the apparently older of the two structures—but somehow it looked like new—the lights were on inside, giving him the impression someone was definitely there. As he got within a few yards of the building, he heard piano music. Sneaking up the front steps in tennis shoes and creeping along the porch, he cautiously peered into one of the floor to ceiling window. With no curtain to block his view, the prissy little miss was sitting at the piano but her hands were in her lap. He'd heard of pianos that played themselves but had never seen one in action. Even covered from head to toe by a heavy housecoat, she was still an attractive and inviting morsel. If he was going to play house with her, he couldn't take a chance on being recognized tomorrow. The ski mask now had a new purpose and would come in handy for a second opportunity for what the resort had to offer him. However—while being extra careful—his new side plan couldn't let anything or anybody come between him and his big payday. Feeling the excitement surge through his body, he'd catch her, do her, and get the hell out of there before her sugar daddy returned.

Boyd wondered where a place like this would have an electrical box. He moved steadily in the continuing rain until finding the back of the building. Along the way, he'd shinned the flashlight against the building, seeing no obvious breaker boxes along the outside walls. Almost on a whim he tried the backdoor, finding it unlocked. What idiots these people are. Don't they realize there are intruders who can rip them off or do worse . . . rape their women? He wanted to laugh, but knew he shouldn't make any noise or his new addition to his plan could be jeopardized.

He snuck quietly inside and painstakingly crept through the house, mindful others beside the girl could be there. Feeling safe while continuing to hear piano music, it dawned on him . . . duh; the sound of music didn't mean she was still sitting there. Stopping now and then to make sure she was still sitting at the piano, he quickly but methodically looked through the house, concluding she was there alone. Good news but still no electrical box. As he inspected the rooms, he'd not noticed anything of real value small enough to carry away, but the furnishings seemed up-town. No use getting side-tracked, he reasoned. He needed to get the power off, get satisfied, and move on. Maybe there was a basement below this old building. If so, perhaps he'd find the breaker box there. He'd go back to the kitchen and start there, looking on the ground floor for a door that didn't lead to another room.

The kitchen turned out to be a good choice, slightly remembering a door off to the side when he'd first entered the house. Gently and slowly opening it, there were steps leading downward. Quietly, yet hastily, he hauled-ass to look at the piano. Good, the young gal was still there and singing along to an old song he'd heard before but couldn't remember the name.

Back in the kitchen again, he looked around one last time and stepped downward. The staircase contained only a small number of stairs and wasn't steep, so it didn't take long to get below and enter a small room with a low ceiling. Although small, it was full of supplies, heavy looking metal tanks, and equipment. Shinning the flashlight along the wall, he spotted the metal doors covering the two electrical breaker boxes.

Approaching the panels, he opened the first one and flipped off the main breaker switch. Still hearing the faint sound of piano music, he moved to the second panel. Having expected the room to be chilly because of its location, it felt downright freezing . . . like a walk-in cooler. But unlike any cooler he'd been in, the air seemed to be moving around him. Frowning, it made no logical sense in an enclosed area. Oh well, he'd soon be leaving . . . looking forward to warming up with the sweetie upstairs. When he flipped the second panel's main switch to off, the music stopped.

When the lights went out and the piano stopped, Ashlynn fumbled in her dad's robe pocket for her phone. Pulling it out, she calmly pushed the lit picture of her dad's face. She was used to the power going out when it rained, so it wasn't a big deal. It happened a lot at home. However, she was relieved when he answered immediately.

"Dad, the power went off. What should I do?"

"I'm just leaving on my way back. Something must have gotten wet and tripped the breaker. Can you find the flashlight in the dark?" Not waiting for a response, he continued, "I think you put both of them in your room."

"I guess so," she answered but not decidedly.

"Do you remember where the electrical room is? It's down the stairs from the kitchen . . . the remodeled cellar. That's where the breaker boxes are. There are two of them. You'll need to check on the one farthest from the stairs. They're just like the ones we have at home, only bigger. Do you remember when I showed you how to tell which one tripped?"

"I'll figure it out. The hardest part will be finding the flashlight," she answered.

"Honey, if you don't want to tackle it, I'll be home in about thirty minutes. Just stay in your room with the flashlight on and wait for me. Okay?"

"Dad . . . just hurry," she answered but already thinking about the best way to navigate in the dark to the main staircase and then upstairs.

Watching for oncoming traffic, Matthew pulled out, seeing the rental car's flashers blinking in the rearview mirror. When back on hard pavement and moving down the road, Brooke looked at him questionably, "What's wrong?"

"The power went off at the manor. I thought we had the problem solved, and I'm pissed." Further explaining his conversation with Ashlynn, he ended with, "Our daughter is a real trouper. She's amazing and more grown-up than we've given her credit. I'm betting the lights will be back on when we get there."

"I only heard snippets of the conversation, but gathered you were talking to Ashlynn when you put my last bag in the car," she replied. "How long before we get there?"

"Probably a half-hour . . . maybe longer. I wish it wasn't raining," he answered.

As soon as the music stopped, Boyd mumbled, "It's show time; I've waited long enough." Hurrying up the stairs, he turned the knob and pushed on the door, but it wouldn't open . . . not even a little bit. Trying it again and thinking it was stuck, he braced his shoulder against the door and thrust his entire weight into it. What the hell, it hadn't budged an inch. Maybe it locked on him, but that didn't seem possible either. Perhaps the door was somehow connected to the power . . . locking automatically in case of fire. It would be a disaster to be found there if the guy came back, deciding to turn on the power and get the heck out of there. Hurrying down the stairs, he jumped the last two steps to get there faster. As he approached the panel boxes, he wondered if he should turn both breakers on or just the last one he'd switched off. Standing in front of the second panel, he heard the above door open and saw light filtering down the stairs through a crack created by the slowly opening door. While amazed and wondering how that was possible, he looked for a place to hide and quickly turned off his flashlight.

Crouched behind a storage shelf and hoping the large boxes blocked his being seen, he waited in fear; a multitude of thoughts rushing through his mind. Expecting the man to be coming down to address the power outage, he was surprised to see the young girl carefully shinning her flashlight on each downward step. Feeling much better because it was her, he could push her aside—unrecognized because of the ski mask—get upstairs, and then get out of the building to freedom. Reminding himself about the possibility of the guy returning at any moment, he'd pressed his luck far enough for a strange piece. He watched her raise the flashlight and move the light across the wall. As soon as the light settled on the opened panel doors, she walked directly toward the second box. Without waiting any longer, he turned on his flashlight and pointed it directly into her eyes.

Blinded by the light, Ashlynn screamed, "Help! Daddy . . . help!"

"Your daddy's not here . . . just me," answered curtly.

"Stay away from me," she shouted.

"Or what? You're gonna hit me with your big bad flashlight," said with a sneer and followed by a guttural chuckle.

Unable to see and terrified, she slowly inched backward, thinking maybe she could run up the stairs and escape before he could catch her. But as the light in her eyes got stronger, she knew he was getting closer. Time stood still, as seconds seemed like forever. How long had it been since she'd talked to her father?

Terror gripping her body and mind, she screamed again, "Stay away from me." Followed instantly by, "Help. Somebody help me."

Suddenly a gust of additional frigid air swirled through the room; the door above slamming shut. And just as abruptly and outside Ashlynn's control, the flashlight was ripped from her hand and flew through the air like a projectile. Instantly and unbelievably, the light from the flashlight began circling, big circles at first, then smaller and smaller ones until the swishing noise stopped, broken by the sound of a loud thud. Not exactly sure where she was in the room, she held her arms out until feeling the wall beside her. Resting her body against the wall for support, she felt physically unbalanced and emotionally drained. Looking down and straining to see in the faint lighting, she saw a motionless figure lying on the floor; his flashlight shining on his legs. She listened for a moment, hearing moaning sounds. While deciding if it was safe enough to run; somehow doubt held her powerless to move. Thinking she should quickly grab for his flashlight, the shelf beside him began to shake. Shivering and feeling her teeth chattering, she slid down the wall's cold surface as the frightening experience continued. What in the world is happening kept going through her mind? The shaking got worse until something big and silver crashed down on him. Immediately, the moaning ceased along with the shaking.

As if caught within a bizarre dream, the freezing wind stopped but the chill in the air remained. And for an instant against the darkness, the young girl in the white nightgown appeared before her. She remained stationary for a few seconds, before swooping away and disappearing. As she left, Ashlynn heard gospel music playing. It was an unknown tune but the words were as clear as if she was sitting in church and listening to the church choir. *"No more pain. No more toil. I'm free to fly. I'm going home to my mansion in the sky."*

Instantaneously, the temperature warmed, and Ashlynn had the feeling of being safe. Watching the still figure on the floor, she moved quickly and grabbed his flashlight. No longer concerned about the power, her only thought was to get upstairs. Bounding up the stairs, she grasped the door handle with trembling fingers, pushing it open easily. Hurrying into the kitchen, she closed the door as quickly as possible. Naturally, she wanted to shut out what had transpired below. As the door clicked shut, she heard her father hollering, "Ashlynn, where are you?"

Answering back, "I'm in the kitchen." Unable to take another step and knowing her father was finally there, she sat down on the kitchen floor and began to cry. Holding the flashlight in her lap, she looked up to see both her dad and mom running toward her. Once by her side, they both knelt down, giving her hugs and kisses.

While stroking Ashlynn's hair, her mother asked, "Honey, did you sleepwalk again?"

"No," she responded without hesitation. Although surprised and happy to see her mom, she looked directly at her dad and said in a composed manner, "Dad, you better call the police. There's a man downstairs in the electrical room. He's under one of those big water tanks. I think he's dead."

Brooke gasped, and Matthew said, "What?"

"Dad, I know it's gonna be hard to believe, but it's the truth. I swear to God. Dad, remember the young girl I saw in the white nightgown; well, she must have known he was coming and wanted to hurt me. That's probably why she wanted to get me out of the manor. Okay here goes. After the power went off, I opened the door to the old cellar and when . . . ."

Made in the USA
San Bernardino, CA
24 June 2016